THE BARBARA CARTLAND ETERNAL COLLECTION

The Barbara Cartland Eternal Collection is the unique opportunity to collect all five hundred of the timeless beautiful romantic novels written by the world's most celebrated and enduring romantic author.

Named the Eternal Collection because Barbara's inspiring stories of pure love, just the same as love itself, the books will be published on the internet at the rate of four titles per month until all five hundred are available.

The Eternal Collection, classic pure romance available worldwide for all time .

I0547506

LOVE LOCKED IN

Barbara Cartland

Barbara Cartland Ebooks Ltd

This edition © 2022

ISBNs

9781788676199   EPUB

9781788676205   PAPERBACK

Book design by M-Y Books
m-ybooks.co.uk

THE LATE DAME BARBARA CARTLAND

Barbara Cartland, who sadly died in May 2000 at the grand age of ninety eight, remains one of the world's most famous romantic novelists. With worldwide sales of over one billion, her outstanding 723 books have been translated into thirty six different languages, to be enjoyed by readers of romance globally.

Writing her first book 'Jigsaw' at the age of 21, Barbara became an immediate bestseller. Building upon this initial success, she wrote continuously throughout her life, producing bestsellers for an astonishing 76 years. In addition to Barbara Cartland's legion of fans in the UK and across Europe, her books have always been immensely popular in the USA. In 1976 she achieved the unprecedented feat of having books at numbers 1 & 2 in the prestigious B. Dalton Bookseller bestsellers list.

Although she is often referred to as the 'Queen of Romance', Barbara Cartland also wrote several historical biographies, six autobiographies and numerous theatrical plays as well as books on life, love, health and cookery. Becoming one of Britain's most popular media personalities and dressed in her trademark pink, Barbara spoke on radio and television about social and political issues, as well as making many public appearances.

In 1991 she became a Dame of the Order of the British Empire for her contribution to literature and her work for humanitarian and charitable causes.

Known for her glamour, style, and vitality Barbara Cartland became a legend in her own lifetime. Best remembered for her wonderful romantic novels and loved by millions of readers worldwide, her books remain treasured for their heroic heroes, plucky heroines and traditional values. But above all, it was Barbara Cartland's overriding belief in the positive power of love to help, heal and improve the quality of life for everyone that made her truly unique.

CHAPTER ONE
1832

The Duchesse de Savigne lifted up her eyes to her cousin.

His Eminence Cardinal de Rochechant was sitting on the other side of the hearth and he asked in a voice that trembled somewhat,

"What has Aristide been doing now?"

"That is what I came to talk to you about, my dear," the Cardinal replied.

"I guessed it," the Duchesse said in a low voice. "I knew that you had not come all this way from Paris just to see me."

The Cardinal smiled.

"That sounds very ungallant. As you know, Louise, I am always anxious to see you when I can spare the time, but I considered that my visit here today, for a very different reason, was urgent."

The Duchesse clasped her blue-veined hands and her rings seemed almost too heavy.

"Tell me the truth, Xavier," she demanded. "In what new scandal is Aristide involved?"

"You really want the truth?" the Cardinal asked.

"I know you intend to reveal it whatever my wishes may be," the Duchesse said with a flash of humour, "so I would like to hear it all without your pretty phrases and without your trying to spare my feelings."

The Cardinal hesitated for a moment before he said almost harshly,

"Aristide is defaming the name of Savigne and is making it a byword for every outrage, scandal and vice."

The Duchesse gave a little gasp, although it was what she had expected to hear and there was a suspicion of tears in her eyes when she said in a low voice that her cousin could hardly hear,

"Tell me – everything."

She had been a very beautiful woman, but constant illnesses had made her face deeply lined and her skin pale to the point of transparency.

She was so thin that she looked as if a puff of wind would blow her away and in fact the Cardinal had been surprised and shocked by her appearance when he arrived at the Château.

He had considered it his duty to come from Paris for the express purpose of asking for the Duchesse's help.

No one knew better than he the damage that the aristocrats like the Duc de Savigne were doing to their country at this particular moment in French history, by their wild extravagance and their exotic parties, which caused growing resentment and disapproval.

'The White Terror' after the Battle of Waterloo had been so insignificant in comparison with the 'Red Revolution' just twenty-three years earlier in 1792. But the rebellion which had taken place only two years ago in 1830 had made the whole country apprehensive.

In protest against the illiberal and reactionary role of King Charles X, rioting had broken out in Paris and the Stock Exchange was set on fire.

The Arsenal and the powder deposit at Salpêtrière fell into insurgent hands. The Louvre and the Tuileries were both taken.

Troops marched into the rebel districts, but they were powerless in narrow streets where the people threw furniture onto their heads.

Six thousand barricades turned most of Paris into an entrenched camp. King Charles X was forced to abdicate and the Duc d'Orléans, Louis-Philippe, a descendant of King Louis XIV was invited to take his place and restore order.

This depended a great deal on regaining the confidence of the people, and the attitude and behaviour of members of the *ancien régime* like the Duc de Savigne were making it far harder than it would have been otherwise.

The Duchesse was waiting and after a moment the Cardinal said,

"It is not only the orgies that Aristide gives or takes part in every evening, it is also the mistresses whom he flaunts in the streets of Paris and the stories of the extravagant presents he gives them, which make those who are living near to starvation restless to say the least of it."

"You are afraid of a recurrence of violence?" the Duchesse asked him quickly.

"There is always the chance it will break out again," the Cardinal replied, "and I consider that to prevent such an explosion it is so essential that the Nobles who have returned to their Château, their estates and rightful place in Society should set an example to those who have suffered so bitterly in the last sixteen years."

"You are right, Xavier," the Duchesse said. "Of course you are right. Have you spoken to Aristide about this?"

The Cardinal gave a little laugh with no humour in it.

"My dear Louise, do you imagine he would listen to me? He has said often enough and publicly, that religion is so out of date. If he has attended Mass in the last ten years I have not heard of it."

The Duchesse put her hands up to her face and they were trembling.

"How could this have – happened to my son of all – people?" she asked almost beneath her breath.

"I suppose it all stems from that regrettable episode in his life," the Cardinal suggested.

The Duchesse did not reply. They were thinking of the tragedy that had overshadowed Aristide's youth and turned him from a charming happy man into a cynic who had gradually become the bitter reactionary that he was now.

"There has been scandal after scandal," the Cardinal related after a moment. "Two weeks ago a young woman, well known in theatrical circles, although I would hesitate to call her an actress, tried to commit suicide."

The Duchesse gave an exclamation of horror, but he continued,

"She made a confession that was printed in every newspaper in France alleging that the cause of her unhappiness was Aristide's callous behaviour towards her."

"She had been his mistress?" the Duchesse enquired.

"One of a dozen others too," he replied. "He apparently had dismissed her in a somewhat cruel fashion and she decided, God help her, that life was not worth living without him."

"Women – always women!" the Duchesse murmured.

The Cardinal was silent for a moment and then he added,

"Aristide is now thirty. It is time he married and produced an heir."

The Duchesse looked at him in a startled fashion as His Eminence continued,

"You know, as well as I do, Louise, that, if there is no direct heir, the title and the estates will go to that elderly cousin who now lives in Montmartre with the artists and has announced quite openly that he is a Republican and disapproves not only of titles but also of personal possessions."

The Duchesse gave a little groan and the Cardinal finished,

"Heaven knows what will happen to the estates if he inherits."

"Does Aristide know this?"

"Of course he knows it," the Cardinal replied, "but, quite frankly, he does not care."

His voice sharpened as he went on,

"I don't think he cares for anything these days not even the women whom he takes up on an impulse and apparently, without any consideration for their feelings, discards them as soon as they bore him."

The Cardinal's lips tightened as he finished,

"And Aristide is very quickly bored!"

"How could we – persuade him to be married? And even if he agreed, would it do any – good?"

"I have no idea," the Cardinal answered. "Frankly I only feel it might be a solution and it might keep him away from Paris. It is all the notoriety that he attracts that is doing so much harm. He is news, Louise, and you know what that means in the 'gutter press'."

The Duchesse gave a deep sigh.

"I have prayed that Aristide would marry and give me a grandson," she said, "or rather many grandchildren. I have always regretted that I was only able to have one child."

"At least Leon died happy, knowing that he had a son," the Cardinal said consolingly.

"He would hardly be happy if he could see him now," the Duchesse replied.

"That is why, Louise, we have to do something."

"You will speak to him on the subject of marriage?"

The Cardinal shook his head.

"No, Louise, *you* must do that."

He rose from the high-backed chair to walk across the room towards the window.

As he moved in his red robes over the exquisite *Savonnerie* carpet, the sunshine coming through the window illuminated the priceless treasures of the Château.

By some miracle the Château Savigne had been spared much of the devastation of the Terror of 1793.

Unlike other Châteaux in the vicinity it had been spared severe looting and the present Duc's grandfather had been far-seeing enough to remove most of the priceless treasures that had been handed down by many generations to a safe place where the Revolutionaries never found them.

Now they had been restored and the Château was, the Cardinal thought, one of the finest in the whole of France.

He may have been prejudiced but he loved the Château Savigne having known it since he was a young man when his beautiful cousin, Louise, had married the reigning Duc.

He looked out now on the great Park with the spotted deer roaming beneath the trees and in the far distance he could see the faint silver of the River Loire as it wound its way through the countryside.

There were great Châteaux on both sides of the river and many others nearby.

When, in the fifteenth century, King Charles VII had been expelled by the English from Paris, he spent much of his time in Tours and in the Châteaux of the surrounding district.

His love for the Province of Touraine was shared by his successors on the Throne during the two subsequent centuries.

The frequent presence of the King in the Loire Valley compelled the Noblemen at Court to follow the Royal example.

For this reason an extraordinary number of Châteaux clustered around the banks of the river and its tributaries.

Huge and majestic Châteaux were erected by the competitive desire of each Nobleman to build a larger and more magnificent house than his neighbour.

Many Châteaux had begun their history as Medieval Fortresses, but with the coming of the Renaissance they were developed into masterpieces of contemporary architecture, ornate and beautiful, which made all those who saw them feel amazed at the wonders in that part of France.

The owners who had fled at the time of the Revolution had returned to set their houses in order, many having the task of completely refurnishing huge, empty and looted rooms.

But whatever effort they have to make, the Cardinal thought, it was worth it and, if they could take so much trouble, why could the Duc de Savigne not follow their example?

He realised that the Duchesse was waiting and he walked back from the window to say,

"There is only one person, Louise, who could make Aristide understand what is required of him and that is you. And you know it."

"But how? Why should he listen to me? He has not done so for many more years than I care to remember."

"I have a feeling, although I might be wrong," the Cardinal said slowly, "that he is still fond of you in his own fashion. If he thought that you were dying, Louise, it might bring him to his senses."

"Dying!" the Duchesse expostulated.

Her eyes met the Cardinal's and, after a long moment, he drew his chair nearer to her and then sat down.

"Now listen to me, Louise – " he began again.

*

The party, which had started quite conventionally, was growing very wild.

The superb dinner for over fifty had made the guests extremely gay and noisy with both sexes flushed and excitable.

The ladies had not left the table and now it was obvious that they were becoming more abandoned, their flirtatious attitudes gave way to a voluptuous enticement that their partners apparently found irresistible.

At the head of the table, seated in a high-backed chair carved with his Coat of Arms, the Duc de Savigne leant back watching those he was entertaining with an enigmatic expression on his face that was hard to read.

Those who knew him very well often wondered how he managed, when he was enjoying himself, to appear in some odd way of his own so aloof and uninterested in everything that was proceeding around him.

On each side of him a beautiful woman, both notorious for their charms, whispered in his ear, showing as they did so an inordinate amount of bare bosom.

The laughter was growing louder until it was superseded by music from the Gallery that overhung the far end of the Banqueting Hall.

The Duc's mansion in Paris was one of the largest and most impressive houses in the *Champs-Élysées*.

Few people passed it without staring with curiosity at its ornate gold-tipped railings and wondering what was taking place in those vast rooms which were described almost daily by reporters who apparently haunted the house in search of a spicy 'titbits' for their newspapers.

Tonight's party, as some Nobleman present thought uncomfortably, would be described in detail in *Le Figaro* and *Le Temps*.

Several of them hoped fervently that their names would not be mentioned, at the same time it was hard to know these days who was in the pay of the Press.

For all they knew, the person who reported this evening's excesses might be one of their own blood or certainly one of their own kind.

"I have something to tell you, Monsieur le Duc," the woman on the Duc's right hand said with pouting lips. "It is wickedly cruel, but it will make you laugh."

"I am waiting," the Duc answered languidly.

"Don't listen to her," the woman on the other side of him interposed. "What she is going to tell you is something about me and I swear to you that it is not true. Promise you will not believe her."

"How can I promise if I have not heard what she has to say?" the Duc asked.

"I assure you it is not credible and what Aimie does not know she invents."

"You must let me be the judge," the Duc insisted.

"Why not?" Rosette asked. "I trust you to find me innocent."

She looked at him provocatively as she spoke and the Duc smiled cynically.

"I doubt if anyone could do that. Rosette! Nevertheless I am prepared to learn about this wicked thing you are alleged to have done."

"I will tell you," Aimie said with some satisfaction.

She bent forward to whisper in his ear and as she did so the music charmed several of the Duc's guests into rising from the table to move onto the polished floor at the end of the room.

The dancing, if that was what it was to be called, was outrageous and was more suitable to a disreputable Dance Hall than to this exclusive neighbourhood of the *Champs-Élysées*.

Except for those indulging in such exuberances, the rest of the guests were too concerned with themselves to be interested and now the women's gowns were slipping from their white shoulders and the men were unbuttoning their waistcoats.

Servants, as if at some previous command, were now busy extinguishing the lights in the chandeliers, leaving only the candles in their sconces and those in the candelabra on the table to light the scene.

It was then that the two women whispering so intimately to the Duc were disturbed by another flamboyant dark-haired beauty who had just electrified Paris by her appearance at the *Théâtre des Variétés*.

She had arrived late at the party after her performance was over and, because dinner had started without her, she had been forced to take a place not at the Duc's side, as she expected, but further down the table.

Now she came up to him and he knew by the expression in her flashing eyes that she was ready to do battle with any rival for his affections.

"Monsieur!" she cried in the light tone of a cooing dove, but with a strong undercurrent of steel, "you are neglecting me!"

"I could never do that for long, Susanne," the Duc replied.

"Then turn *cette canaille* away and give me your attention," Susanne replied.

Aimie and Rosette looked at her angrily and she went on,

"Have they anything to offer you, you who would seek perfection and boast that you are a *connoisseur*?"

The Duc looked amused, but he did not answer.

"If it was a question of the judgement of Paris," she said, "there would, I know, be no doubt to whom you would award the golden apple."

"That may be your opinion, Susanne," Aimie said sharply, "but it is not ours!"

Susanne looked her up and down scornfully.

"You are intruding, Susanne," Rosette said. "We are entertaining Monsieur and it is not very amusing for him or for us to listen to you crowing about yourself like a cock on a dung-hill."

Susanne struck an attitude that was dramatic and at the same time aggressive. She looked at the Duc and the expression in her eyes challenged him.

"It is up to you, *monsieur*," she said softly – and there was an invitation even in the movement of her lips.

Both Aimie and Rosette looked at him too and now there was no mistaking that all three women were waiting breathlessly for his verdict.

"If my knowledge of mythology is not at fault," the Duc replied slowly after a moment, "when Paris was asked to judge between the Goddesses they did exhibit *all* their charms."

There was a moment's pause and then Susanne with a little laugh slipped her gown from her shoulders and then both Aimie and Rosette followed her example.

The Duc made no movement only after a second or two he asked lazily,

"And the golden apple means?"

"Of course, it is to spend the night with you, *monsieur*," Susanne pointed out.

Again there was a pause as the Duc looked at the three women standing in front of him, each proudly confident that she would be the winner.

There was little to choose between them, perhaps Susanne's waist was a little smaller, but her thigh was thicker than Rosette's. While Aimie's breasts were fuller.

At last the Duc said, his voice still languid but with a touch of amusement in it,

"The only Diplomatic decision I can make is to divide the prize of myself in equal parts. Fortunately my bed is large enough!"

There was then a shriek of astonishment, but it was very obvious that the ladies accepted the suggestion without reserve.

The Duc glanced at his guests and realised that what the newspapers would undoubtedly declaim as 'an exotic orgy reminiscent of Roman times' was now taking place.

Raising her fallen garments and holding them across her breasts, Susanne bent towards him.

"Why are we waiting?" she asked.

The Duc met her glance and replied with a twist of his lips,

"You are impatient, Susanne, but then you have always been the same."

"I am impatient for you," she answered. "I am prepared to show these little rats from the sewers that they are both stupid and ignorant in *les sciences galantes*."

The Duc was about to reply when a powdered footman dressed up in the scarlet and gold Savigne Livery stood at his side.

"This has just arrived by special courier, *Monsieur le Duc*," he said and held out a silver salver on which lay a letter.

The Duc looked at it indifferently and then seemed about to wave the man away until the footman added,

"The man came from the Château Savigne, *Monsieur le Duc*."

The Duc sat up in his chair and took the letter from the salver.

He opened it, read what was written and rose to his feet.

Without a word to the three women awaiting his commands and without even looking at them, he turned and walked from the room followed by his servant.

*

His Eminence, Cardinal de Rochechant, as he drove along the rough roads thought as he had thought so often that there was nothing more beautiful than what was then known as

'The Garden of France'.

It was not only the Châteaux that were so impressive but the Atlantic breezes penetrated as far as Tours, which was about two hundred kilometres from the sea and created conditions of life rarely found so far inland.

Because of the configuration of the valley, so wide and fertile, it had also been called the 'Smile of France', the smile reminiscent of that on the face of the Mona Lisa.

This name had reason, since Leonardo da Vinci spent his last two years in the valley of the Loire in a small Château close to Amboise.

Since then more romance had in the course of centuries taken place on the banks of the Loire than on any river in the world.

Soon, the Cardinal reflected, the dry months of the summer would divide the waters into many little streams, which would flow green and pellucid amongst the sandbanks and narrow islands. They would be covered with the tangles of the olive-green willow that always thrived in this watery soil.

The vineyards on the gentle slopes of the valley produced the delectable light wines that the Cardinal found he enjoyed more than any of the full-bodied wines from other districts. But as it happened he was at the moment not concerned with the beauty of the Loire Valley, which always moved him, but with the news that he had received this morning.

It had arrived at the Château de Blois where he was staying, having deliberately delayed his return to Paris until the information he required came from the Duchesse.

Blois had been a Royal residence and the Cardinal was comfortable there, but he found it difficult to think about anything except the drama which he was aware was taking place at Château Savigne.

Almost clairvoyantly he imagined that the Duc on receiving his mother's letter had set off from Paris with all possible speed to go to her side.

The Duchesse had in fact written exactly the letter that the Cardinal had suggested to her.

"May 12th, 1852. Château Savigne.

My dearest son,

I am in ill health and I feel I am not long for this world. I beg you to visit me as soon as it is possible, for I could not bear to die without seeing your dear face once again and hearing your voice.

If it is inconvenient for you to leave Paris at this moment, you must forgive me, but my heart yearns for you and I shall pray that God will let me remain in this world long enough to hold you in my arms before He takes me into His care.

I remain, my dearest and most beloved Aristide,

Your loving mother,

Louise de Savigne."

The Duc did not wait for his carriage or for the innumerable retinues of valets and other servants with whom he always travelled in a state that was almost like a Royal progress.

Instead, accompanied only by his Comptroller and two grooms, he left Paris as dawn was breaking and set off across country towards Tours.

The Duc's Comptroller was in fact a personal friend, one of the few he admitted to such intimacy.

Pierre de Bethune was the impoverished younger son of a Nobleman who had lost his life and everything he possessed during the Revolution.

The Duc had found Pierre, eking out a precarious existence in the more sordid nightspots of Paris and had offered him a post in his household.

Pierre had rewarded him with a unique devotion which surprised other men of the Duc's acquaintance and became in fact not only his constant companion but also his confidant.

They rode swiftly and without speaking for some time.

Then Pierre, turning to his employer, said with a smile,

"This sweeps away the cobwebs, does it not, *monsieur*?"

"That was just what I was thinking myself," the Duc replied.

Dawn was rising, turning the countryside to gold and, if the Duc found it different from the usual debris of a dissolute evening or an untidy bedroom strewn with female garments, he did not say so.

His Comptroller thought that some lines of dissipation marked on his Master's face were lightening. It might have been the effect dawn, but he did not look so bored or so cynical.

"You realise, *monsieur*," Pierre de Bethune said, "that this will be the first time I have visited the Château Savigne?"

"The first time?" the Duc mused. "Well, I will wonder what you will think of it, a great Barrack of a place, although I think it has a certain charm."

He did not elaborate on what this was and, having ridden hard all day, they then slept the night in an uncomfortable hostel.

After an indifferent dinner, although the wine was good, Pierre de Bethune started to talk of the Château.

"Why do you so seldom go there, monsieur?" he enquired.

"I should have thought it obvious," the Duc replied uncompromisingly. "It bores me!"

"I am surprised at that," Pierre said. "You love riding and who can ride in real comfort in Paris? And I feel, although you have never said so, that you are fond of the country."

"It is dull I tell you," the Duc said almost sharply. "*Deadly dull!* And as you well know, Pierre, the one thing I try to avoid is boredom."

'Tell me about your home."

"What do you want to know?" the Duc enquired. "That it has turrets and towers, that it is in such a sheltered position that palm trees grow in the garden that Louis XVI slept there and his bedroom, which I use, is unchanged?"

"It sounds so fascinating," Pierre said, "and I suspect, although you will not admit it, that you loved it when you were young."

For a moment the Duc seemed to be very still and then he said,

"It is so long ago that I have forgotten."

But Pierre de Bethune knew that he lied.

They arrived at Savigne early in the morning and the Duc had been right, Pierre thought, in describing his house as having towers and turrets.

Never had he seen anything so attractive or so fairytale-like as the great Château with its gardens sloping down to the banks of the river and its roofs and chimneys silhouetted against the blue sky.

The Duc rode up to the front door where the grooms were waiting to take his horse and he walked up the broad steps through a line of bowing servants.

"May I welcome you, *Monsieur le Duc*?" the Clerk of Chambers asked.

"Take me to *Madame la Duchesse*," the Duc replied.

The Clerk of Chambers went ahead of him up the curving carved staircase and along the broad corridor to the South wing occupied by his mother ever since she had been widowed.

A maid opened the door, dropping a respectful curtsey and the Duc strode in, pulling off his gloves as he did so. The Duchesse was lying in a huge canopied bed.

She looked extremely frail amongst the lace-edged pillows and the ermine cover was no whiter than the pallor of her face.

"My son!"

She held out her hands to him and the Duc took them in both of his, kissing them gently.

Like the Cardinal he was shocked by the difference in her appearance since he had last seen her and she seemed to have become almost disembodied and already part of the spiritual world.

"I came the moment I received your letter, Mama."

"Thank you – my dearest," the Duchesse said. "I have been praying that you would be – in time."

"You have seen the best Doctors? Is there nothing they can do for you?"

"Nothing, my dearest, and please don't you grieve for me. I shall be with your father as I have longed to be ever since he left me.

The Duc's fingers tightened on hers.

The maid closed the door and they were alone in the room.

"There is one thing I would – ask of you," the Duchesse said in a low voice, "just one thing – Aristide before I – die."

"What is it, Mama?"

There was an expression in the Duc's eyes that told her that he almost anticipated what she had to say.

"I cannot die in – peace unless I know that the – succession is – assured."

The Duc drew in his breath.

"It is time that you married, my beloved son," the Duchesse said, "and I want more than I have ever wanted anything in my whole life to hold – your son in my arms."

"It is impossible, Mama!"

"But why? " the Duchesse asked.

He did not reply and after a moment she said brokenly,"

Oh, Aristide, you were such a sweet and charming little boy and we loved you so deeply – your father and I."

Her fingers tightened again on his as she went on,

"When you grew older, we were very proud of you. You had every talent and you were so strong and athletic, which delighted your father."

The Duc moved a little restlessly.

"Then you have changed. The son who we knew and loved went away from me. I have thanked God many times that your father is not here to see the alteration."

"There is nothing that can be done about it, my Mama. I am as I am and as far as I am concerned, I am content."

"Is that really true?" the Duchesse asked anxiously.

She looked as she spoke at the lines on his face, which seemed to be those of discontent already etched from his nose to his mouth and the dark blue shadows of dissipation under his eyes.

Once, the Duchesse often thought despairingly, he had been the best-looking young man anyone could find in the whole length and breadth of France.

Now he appeared older than his years and he looked like a man who had drunk of the very dregs of life and found them sour.

"Please – Aristide," she urged him almost beneath her breath.

He rose from the side of her bed to walk away across the room.

On the opposite wall were a number of miniatures, all exquisitely painted, of the Ducs de Savigne down the ages.

They were indeed a handsome lot, ending with his father, whose features were very like his own, except that there was a nobility about his expression that was inescapable.

He stood there with his back to the bed and after a moment the Duchesse could no longer look at him.

She knew that she had failed and closed her eyes. The Cardinal had been wrong.

Aristide no longer cared for her. They had not even the natural affection of a mother and a son left between them.

'I want to die,' she told herself, 'and there is no pretence about that. I shall die because I have nothing left to live for.'

She had known all through the pain and discomfort she suffered especially in the winter that the one thing that kept her going was the thought that one day her son would come back to her.

One day he would live here at the Château and the empty corridors would come alive and the great rooms would be filled with the sound of voices and the laughter of children.

But now she knew that it was only a dream, a dream that would never materialise, it was something that she had merely conjured up, the sick fancy of an ill woman.

The Duc had finished his inspection of the family portraits that gleamed against the blue damask walls, their exquisitely jewelled frames glittering in the sunshine.

He walked back towards the bed and stood looking down at his mother.

She did not open her eyes and, because she was so still, he had a sudden fear that she was no longer breathing.

"Mama!"

It was a call, an urgent call, and despondently she opened her eyes.

"I will do as you ask!"

"Aristide. Do you mean – that?"

"If it will make you happy."

"You know it will make me happier than I can ever tell you."

"Then it will be worth all the boredom and depression that it will bring me."

"Thank you, my darling. Now I have something to live for, although I don't think that I shall linger long."

"You will have to live," the Duc said, "because this is your idea and I leave it entirely in your hands."

The Duchesse looked startled.

"You mean – ?" she began.

"I mean," the Duc interrupted, "that I will personally take no initiative. Choose my wife yourself. I am sure she will prove very suitable. Arrange the marriage. It will have to be here in our own Chapel so that you can see me suitably shackled in Holy wedlock. You would not be well enough to travel elsewhere."

"But, Aristide – !"

"Those are my conditions," the Duc then stipulated. "I do not wish to see the girl or have anything to do with her until she is my wife. Then I will come here from Paris and stay long enough to breed the grandson you so fervently desire."

"But, dearest – " the Duchesse said again.

"I don't intend to argue about it," the Duc stated. "You have gained your way, Mama, and I have a suspicion that you were quite certain you would do so. Be content!"

The Duchesse put out her hands to touch his.

"I want you to be – happy," she said in a low voice.

The Duc's lips twisted.

"Is that why you brought me here?"

"That is what I believe marriage will give you. I was, as you know, very happy with your father and he with me."

"But I am not my father and never will be," the Duc said, "and you are very unlikely to find me a wife as charming and as beautiful as you, Mama."

"I shall try, my dearest, I shall try hard. But it will be a difficult if you will not help me and make yourself pleasant."

"I daresay that my wife, when I do have one, will not find me unpleasant," the Duc said mockingly. "There are quite a number of women who appear to enjoy my company."

"What sort of women?" the Duchesse asked gently.

The Duc raised her hand to his lips.

"We have struck a bargain, Mama, you and I, and I have no wish to discuss it further. Now, if you will forgive me, I wish to bathe and change my clothes."

"I am deeply grateful for your coming when I wanted you," the Duchesse smiled.

"I have a feeling, Mama, that you are much stronger than you appear. Your willpower at any rate has not diminished in its strength and determination."

"I only want your happiness," she murmured again.

"I wonder what that elusive condition is really like?" the Duc mused. "Somehow I don't seem to have encountered it for so long that I have forgotten how to recognise it."

"Oh, Aristide – !"

There was a little throb in the Duchesse's voice and the Duc said quickly,

"We are becoming absurdly sentimental. Make your plans, Mama, and, as I have already promised, I will acquiesce in them. Don't let us bore ourselves by discussing them further."

He rose as he spoke.

For a moment he looked down at her and then bent forward and kissed her on the cheek.

"Keep alive, Mama," he said quietly. "I have a distinct feeling that Savigne will crumble into ruins without your being here."

He walked from the room and, having watched him go, the Duchesse lay back against her pillows feeling suddenly exhausted.

The Cardinal had been right, she thought. Aristide did still care for her and, because she had asked it of him, he had agreed to be married.

It was a swifter victory than she hoped for and at the same time she was apprehensive.

What woman would find him a congenial husband in the mood he was in now?

The Duchesse had not missed the underlying bitterness, the irony and the cynicism in his voice when he promised to do what she wished.

Then she told herself that all that really mattered was that there should be an heir.

She faced the fact that Aristide, once the honeymoon, if it could be so called, was over he would doubtless return to the fast life that he enjoyed so much in Paris.

She doubted, however optimistic the Cardinal might be, that a wife, or even a family, would change him back into a respectable landowner directing his country possessions as the King and the new Régime thought so desirable.

Equally the first step had been taken and Aristide had agreed to be married and now the question was to find him a suitable wife.

The Duchesse reached out her hand for the gold bell that stood by her bedside.

Almost immediately the door opened and one of her lady's maids came into the room.

"Bring my writing paper, inkpot and pen," the Duchesse commanded. "And tell a groom to be ready to take a message immediately to His Eminence the Cardinal at Blois."

The maid curtseyed.

"I'll do that, *Madame*."

'The Cardinal will be delighted,' the Duchesse thought to herself.

When he had suggested what she should say, she had been almost sure that his optimism was unfounded and that Aristide would not respond.

But in fact he had come to Savigne at a moment's notice, riding all the way and, because he believed that she might die, he had surrendered his freedom without even a struggle.

'God help him – *God help my son*,' the Duchesse prayed.

It was a prayer that she had repeated and repeated over the years and she had begun to feel that God was not interested in her pleas and had turned away from her.

Now everything had changed and, as the maid returned with her writing materials, she sat up in bed and took the white quill-pen in her hand.

*

In the carriage His Eminence the Cardinal opened the Duchesse's letter and read it again.

He could hardly believe that Aristide had given his mother such a completely free hand in choosing him a bride and that he would take no personal part in it.

But there it was clearly written in the Duchesse's elegant handwriting.

Now the Cardinal drew another piece of paper from the pocket of his crimson robes.

On it were jotted down the names that he and the Duchesse had discussed together as being suitable brides for the Duc de Savigne.

While he had been at the Château Blois, the Cardinal had taken the opportunity of very discreetly sounding out his host about the girls whose family names were written on the list.

He had chosen his words with care.

"Do you often see the Duc de Foucauld-Fleury?" he asked.

"He and his family are frequently here," was the answer.

"Does that mean he has a large family?"

"Yes, indeed, although most of them are married."

"Of course, I remember. His son made an excellent alliance. I believe I met his wife in Paris."

"There is only one of the Duc's seven children who is still unwed."

"I think I heard somewhere that her name is 'Isabelle'," the Cardinal murmured a little vaguely.

"Your Eminence is right. An attractive girl. I am surprised that she has not yet married, but apparently the young gentleman who she was more or less affianced to three years ago was regrettably killed in an accident."

"That was unfortunate," the Cardinal replied.

"Very, but I expect the Duc will be finding a husband for her soon."

The Cardinal changed the subject. He had found out what he wanted to know.

Later on he questioned his host about the Marquis d'Urville and found that his daughter, Henriette, was just eighteen and noted as being a beauty.

There was only one other name on the list, but, as both the Cardinal and the Duchesse were certain that they would have to look no further than the Duc's Château or the Marquis's Château to find a suitable bride, he ignored it.

'Whatever she is like,' the Cardinal told himself, 'it is unlikely that the wretched girl will be able to hold the affections of Aristide for long.'

He sighed.

"But at least he could offer her an ancient name written into the history of France, great possessions and a sublime Château without its peer in the district including Chambord and Chenonceaux."

They were near Chenonceaux at the moment and he leaned out of his carriage to look at the famous building, which had belonged to the most beautiful woman that France had ever known.

Diane de Poitiers had been twenty years older than King Henry II, but he loved her until he died and a contemporary wrote that, when she was nearly sixty-seven, she was as beautiful to look at and as attractive as she had been at thirty.

Of course, the Cardinal now reflected, the Count had implied that Diane used witchcraft to keep her loveliness and it was reported that she took some special sort of broth every day, which rendered her immune from the encroaches of time.

The Cardinal, however, a keen historian and a man of intelligence, had always thought that one of the reasons why Diane de Poitiers kept her looks until she was an old woman was the fact that she always bathed in cold water and never partook of rich food and the profusion of wines that were to be found at the King's table.

He could see Chenonceaux now clearly and the unusual manner in which it was built on two piers of a former mill resting on the bed of the River Cher.

There was a two-storeyed Gallery on the long bridge over the river and, reflected in the still water, it looked romantic and very beautiful.

'That,' the Cardinal said to himself with a sudden unusual twist of imaginative fancy, 'is how a woman should look, beautiful and at the same time excitingly original with perhaps a touch of mystery and excitement about her so that a man would never be bored.'

The word inevitably brought him back to the Duc.

He had a feeling that the woman who could divert the Duc from the excesses with which he relieved his *ennui* had not yet been born!

CHAPTER TWO

His Eminence the Cardinal, driving through the sunlit countryside, was deep in thought.

He was wondering how he could explain to the Duchesse that he had failed in the quest that she had sent him on.

He had never imagined for a moment that he would not succeed in obtaining the consent of one of the young women she had chosen to become the bride of the Duc de Savigne.

He had thought the most suitable one would prove to be Isabelle, the daughter of the Duc de Foucauld-Fleury.

He had arrived at the Duc's Château to be greeted enthusiastically by both the Duc and the Duchesse who were devout Catholics.

"It is far too long, Your Eminence, since we have had the pleasure of welcoming you to this part of the country," the Duc said genially.

"My duties in Paris do unfortunately keep me fully occupied there," the Cardinal replied, "but I assure you, *monsieur*, it is a very great pleasure for me to be in Touraine again."

"And it is certainly a pleasure for us," the Duc answered.

The Cardinal enjoyed an excellent luncheon and noted with satisfaction that Isabelle was an attractive young woman with plenty of common sense and by no means untalented.

'She would certainly make Aristide a commendable wife,' he reflected.

After luncheon the Duc took the Cardinal into his private study, which was but one of the most magnificent and impressive rooms in the Château.

"I would fancy, Your Eminence," he said, "that you have a special reason for calling on me. When I received your message from Blois, I had the feeling, although I may be wrong, that it was not entirely for the pleasure of my company that you wished to come here."

The Cardinal smiled.

"You are very perceptive, *Monsieur le Duc*, and in fact you are right. I have an ulterior motive for my visit."

"I was sure of it," the Duc said, "although I have no idea what it can be."

The Cardinal paused a moment before he said,

"I am empowered by the Duchesse de Savigne and by her son, the Duc, to suggest that a liaison between your two families might be to the advantage of the young people concerned."

He was watching the Duc as he spoke and saw him stiffen.

For a moment there was an almost incredulous look in his eyes.

Then, when he seemed to be feeling for words, the door opened and Isabelle came in.

"Forgive me, *mon père,* if I interrupt you and His Eminence, but you left your spectacles in the dining room and I thought that you might need them."

She put them on a small table by her father's chair. He looked at her, then as she turned to leave the room, he said,

"Wait, Isabelle! I was just about to tell His Eminence that I have agreed to your marriage with Michel de Croix and that it will take place in the autumn."

For a moment Isabelle's eyes widened as if she could not believe what she was hearing. Then a look of radiance seemed to transform her face into unexpected beauty.

"Do you mean that, Papa?" she asked in a low voice.

"But of course!" the Duc replied. "As I was going to inform His Eminence, your mother and I are satisfied that Michel de Croix is exactly the husband who we feel that you will be happy with."

The Cardinal was an intuitive man. He knew quite well that the Duc had only made up his mind at this precise moment that his daughter should marry a man whose eligibility had been hotly contested until the suggestion of another alliance had decided the issue.

It was a blow that he had not expected, but the Cardinal reacted like a trained Diplomat.

He managed to congratulate Isabelle and give her his Blessing on her coming nuptials with what passed for a note of sincerity in his voice.

"I must regret, Your Eminence," the Duc said when Isabelle had left the room, "that your journey has been for nothing."

"I would not say that," the Cardinal replied. "I have greatly enjoyed meeting you again, *Monsieur le Duc,* and I hope that it will not be long before I have the pleasure of entertaining you in Paris."

"You are very gracious," the Duc replied.

Their eyes met and they totally understood each other. Both knew without expressing it in words exactly what had taken place.

As the Cardinal drove away and he metaphorically crossed the Duc's daughter off his list, he wondered for the first time if his task might not be as easy as he and the Duchesse had anticipated.

He had assumed that the main hurdle would be to persuade the Duc to marry, but now it seemed, if the Duc de Foucauld-Fleury was anything to go by, that it might just prove more difficult to find a bride.

The Marquis d'Urville made no pretence of hiding his real feelings, nor did he doll them up as the Duc had done with what the Cardinal told himself were 'pretty ribbons'.

"Allow Henriette to marry de Savigne!" he exclaimed at once. "Your Eminence must be deranged if you think for one moment that I would entrust any woman, let alone my daughter, to that lecher, that young swine who has made the name de Savigne a byword in the gutters of Paris!"

The Marquis was a stout man and he grew so crimson in the face at the very idea that the Cardinal was afraid that he might have a stroke.

"It was but a suggestion, my dear Marquis," he said soothingly.

"A suggestion that never should have been made to me," the Marquis stormed. "Does the *Duchesse* think I am deaf? That I do not hear the stories that are told about her son? That I am blind so that I cannot read the newspapers?"

He paused for breath before he added,

"If you will ask me, Your Eminence is wasting your time. No father worthy of his name would permit one of his daughters to enter the Château Savigne, let alone marry its owner. I personally would rather see my child dead!"

'That was certainly plain speaking,' the Cardinal told himself, as he drove away from the Château and so he envisaged that the Vicomte de Boulaincourt's answer might well be the same before he discovered on arrival that his daughter's engagement had been announced the previous week.

He would, however, have been very obtuse if he had not realised that the Vicomte was relieved that he was not put in the unpleasant position of having to refuse an alliance with the House of Savigne.

"I expect you left Paris, Your Eminence, before the Notice of Engagement appeared in several of the newspapers," he said. "It is in fact a marriage on which my wife and I set our hearts many years ago and it is extremely satisfactory to realise that both my daughter and her fiancé are very much in love with each other."

Again the Cardinal gave everybody concerned his Blessing. Then he was driving away over dusty roads knowing that now he had nowhere to go but the Château

Savigne to report the complete and utter failure of his mission.

'There must be other young ladies,' he tried to tell himself optimistically.

Then he remembered that the Duchesse had gone carefully over the list of eligible young women in the district.

Now the only thing to do, the Cardinal thought, was to go further afield, perhaps to the South of France, the West or even North where the name of Savigne would mean something different to what it meant in a Province that was so close to Paris.

He only hoped that the Duchesse would not insist on his making the journey in person to visit such families.

He was not only extremely busy in Paris, he was also extremely comfortable there and he found it tiring to be bumping over dusty roads and sleeping in unfamiliar beds.

'I should never have become involved in this,' he thought with a touch of irritability.

But then he knew that, because he was related to the Duchesse and, because he had been extremely fond of the last Duc, his conscience would not allow him to rest until he had tried by every means in his power to save their son from himself.

Because it came naturally to him he said a prayer that some way might be found to help a sinner who at least in God's sight would not be beyond redemption.

Then almost as if in answer to his prayer, he saw as the carriage drove by a signpost at the corner of a road, which read, "*Monceau-sur-Indre 5 Kilometres*".

The Cardinal put up his hand.

"Stop the carriage!" he commanded.

His Chaplain, sitting opposite to him, a most earnest young man, but pale and somewhat cadaverous-looking from over-fasting, jerked to attention.

"Stop the carriage, *Monseigneur*?" he questioned in surprise.

"You heard what I said!" the Cardinal answered and the Chaplain obeyed his order.

The six horses were pulled to a standstill and one of the outriders wearing the Cardinal's colourful Livery came riding to the open window.

"You require something, Your Eminence?"

"Turn the horses round," the Cardinal ordered, "and take me to the Château Monceau. It is at the end of the village beyond the Church."

"Very good, Your Eminence."

With some difficulty the heavy carriage was turned a little way down the road and the cavalcade started back, turning down the narrow way towards the small village of Monceau.

The Cardinal had been right in saying that the Château was easy to find.

Beyond the Church there was a pair of wrought-iron gates, sadly in need of paint, and a short drive where the trees had overgrown so that they formed a green tunnel whose branches occasionally swept the top of the carriage.

At the end of it was the Château with its pointed turrets and dormer windows.

Its Gothic symmetry was reflected in a small stream which, at one side of the Château, had broadened into a lake.

The trees had grown round the house until its Greystone was framed and almost enclosed by them.

Looking at it as they turned on the unkempt gravel sweep in front of the porticoed door, the Cardinal thought it looked even more like the Château of *The Sleeping Beauty* than when he had last seen it.

Knowing that they were not expected to arrive here, the Chaplain looked at the Cardinal for instructions.

"Enquire if the Comte de Monceau is at home," he ordered and the Chaplain alighted from the carriage just as the door was opened by an elderly servant.

The Chaplain returned to the carriage.

"The servant said that the Comte is in his library, Your Eminence, and he has gone to inform him of your arrival."

The Cardinal alighted and then walked slowly up the steps. Only as he reached the top of them did a man come hurrying through the hall, both hands outstretched in welcome.

"Xavier!" he called. "This is a most delightful surprise!"

He reached the Cardinal's side, clasped both his hands and then, as if he had remembered his rank, genuflected and kissed his ring.

"My dear Gérard," the Cardinal said. "I was passing the end of the road to the village and suddenly realised how long it was since we last saw each other."

"Come in! Come into the library," the Comte said. "We will drink a glass of wine and you must tell me all that has happened to you since we last met."

"That will take time," the Cardinal replied with a smile.

"You will stay to dinner, or the night, if it pleases you?"

"I am expected at the Château de Savigne, but dinner, if we could have it early, Gérard, would be most pleasant."

The Comte made a sound that was a wordless expression of joy and, having shown the Cardinal into the library, hurried to the door to give the order for the servant to bring wine.

He crossed the room to look at the Cardinal who had seated himself on one of the few available chairs. Everywhere else there were books.

Never had he thought it possible in all his experience to find so many books accumulated in one room, large though it was.

Not only were the walls covered with them, but there were great piles in every corner, on every table, on every chair and it was very obvious that before he arrived the Comte had been working at his desk.

It was strewn with manuscripts and also with books, some open, many with small pieces of paper sticking out of their leaves to mark a special place.

When the Comte reached the Cardinal's side, he looked up at him and said,

"Let me look at you, Gérard. You have certainly changed very little since the days when we enjoyed life together."

"It was a long time ago," the Comte remarked.

He was in fact a very handsome man, although untidily dressed as if he found anything that kept him from his books irksome and looked far younger than his years.

There was a little grey now in his hair, while the Cardinal's was almost white. His eyes sparkled when he talked and his lips smiled spontaneously.

"Tell me about yourself, Xavier," he said. "I know how important you have become and what a great Power you are in Paris."

"I wish that was true," the Cardinal said with a sigh, "very few people today listen to the Church."

"I believe that is so," the Comte agreed, "but I always knew, Xavier, in those days when we were both students struggling to acquire knowledge, that you would reach the heights, while I – "

He made a gesture towards his desk.

"You have had a book published, I believe," the Cardinal queried.

"Two, as it happens," the Comte replied, "but who reads them? People are not interested in the past. They are too busy living in the present."

"Nevertheless, whatever happens in the world, scholars and those who record history are a necessity for future generations," the Cardinal said quietly. "When I die, I shall doubtless be forgotten, while you, Gérard, will be read perhaps many centuries into the future."

The Comte laughed and it was a boyish sound.

"You are just the same, Xavier, forever inspiring those who will listen to you. I shall always remember your first sermons in that dingy little Church in the slums of Montparnasse. You started out with, was it twelve, in the congregation and ended up with being unable to get everyone inside the building!"

The Cardinal gave another sigh.

"It was hard work, Gérard, but I think sometimes that I have never been so happy."

There was something in the way he spoke that made the Comte look at him sharply and say,

"You chose a hard road when you decided to renounce the usual blessings of mankind a home, a wife and children. I admired you for it then, Xavier, and I still admire you now."

A servant came into the library to set down a bottle of wine and two glasses.

He had difficulty in finding room on the table for the salver, but finally he compromised by putting it on top of several books.

The Cardinal noted with pleasure that it was a local wine that he had a strong partiality for and when the glass was handed to him he sipped it appreciatively before he said,

"Tell me, Gérard, about yourself. I was sure that you would be happy in your marriage, although I could not attend the Wedding."

"I quite understood that you were too busy to spare the time," the Comte said. "Do you realise, Xavier, that it is twenty years since we have seen each other? And yet I remember so many things we used to talk about."

"As if it was yesterday," the Cardinal murmured as if to himself.

"I wish you had known Fleur," the Comte said. "She was not only beautiful but also very intelligent. She helped me with my books, she made my life a Paradise that is not granted to many men in this world."

"She is no longer with you?" the Cardinal enquired.

"She died nearly three years ago," the Comte answered.

There was a note in his voice that told the Cardinal of the agony he must have passed through on losing his beloved.

"I am deeply sorry," the Cardinal said. "And I am sorry too that I did not realise you had been bereaved. I would gladly have come to see you and tried to bring you a little comfort."

At the same time he wondered if in fact he was telling the truth.

Would he really have left his many commitments in Paris and journeyed to Touraine just to succour a friend, even Gérard de Monceau who had meant so much to him in his youth?

"There was nothing anyone could do," the Comte said, "and Syrilla was with me, thank God!"

"Syrilla?" the Cardinal questioned.

"My daughter," the Comte explained. "We did think when she was born that we might ask you to christen her, but already you had become famous, Xavier. You had already begun to move up the ladder towards your present position."

The Comte smiled before he added,

"We often talked of you, my wife and I, and she was always interested in how much our friendship had meant to me when we were young. We quiet countryfolk could not presume to intrude into the world of affairs where you play such a vital role."

"Tell me about Syrilla," the Cardinal suggested.

There was a sudden light in the Comte's eyes as he said,

"She is lovely in mind, body and soul. I will show you a portrait of her that has recently been executed by a young artist who was on his holiday in the village. He asked permission to paint Syrilla and I think it is an excellent likeness."

He rose to walk across the library to where, in a far corner almost obscured by books, the Cardinal could see that there was an unframed canvas standing on a low easel.

The Comte had just picked it up in his hands when through the long window that opened into the garden there appeared a slender figure in a white gown.

The girl ran across the room and, as she did so, the Cardinal thought that she moved with an unusual grace.

It was almost as if she floated, her feet hardly touching the ground with her full skirts brushing against the piles of books as she passed them.

"Papa," she said in a lilting voice that was also musical. "I have something so exciting to tell you!"

"What is it, my dearest?" the Comte asked.

"I was with Jacques in the Park while he was tending the baby lambs that have just been born when something quite extraordinary happened."

"What was it?" the Comte asked.

"One of them, when he picked it up from the grass, appeared to be dead, in fact I thought there was no hope for it. Then Jacques held it in his arms, opened its mouth and blew into it. He blew hard, Papa, giving his breath, as it were, to the lamb, and you will hardly believe this but it came alive!"

"That certainly sounds extraordinary," the Comte nodded.

"It *was* extraordinary!" Syrilla said. "Do you think it possible that we ourselves can give life to those who need it?"

"Life comes from God," the Cardinal interposed, "but sometimes we have the privilege of transmitting it to others."

Syrilla started as he spoke and turned round to look at him, having had, he knew, no idea that there was anyone else in the room except for her father.

Now the Cardinal saw that she was very lovely, at the same time quite unlike anything he had expected.

For one thing she was fair. Her hair was golden and her eyes were very blue and her skin was white with just a touch of colour on the cheeks.

She was small and exquisitely made and, as she moved towards him, he realised again that she had a grace that he had seldom seen in any young woman except perhaps a ballerina.

"This is my daughter, Syrilla, Xavier," the Comte said proudly.

Syrilla sank down in front of the Cardinal and kissed the great emerald ring he wore.

"Forgive me, Your Eminence," she said. "I had no idea that Papa has a visitor."

"I am an old friend," the Cardinal replied, "and it is so remiss of me that I did not know of your existence until a few moments ago."

Syrilla smiled and he noticed that she had a dimple on each side of her mouth.

"I do know who you are," she said, "because Papa has so often spoken of you. What fun you must have had when you were students together."

"We did indeed," he replied, "and it is my loss that your father and I have almost lost touch with each other."

"Now you are here," Syrilla said softly, "may I look at your horses? For I feel sure that Your Eminence will have arrived with an impressive entourage."

"I am sure they will be as delighted as I am to make your acquaintance," the Cardinal replied.

"Before you become immersed in His Eminence's horseflesh that you forget everything else," the Comte said, "will you tell Cook that His Eminence will be staying for dinner and she must do her best at such short notice. We must also dine early."

"You cannot stay the night?" Syrilla asked the Cardinal.

"I am afraid not, but I shall look forward to dining with you and your father."

"It will be so exciting for us," Syrilla said, "but don't be disappointed with what you may find very simple fare."

She gave him a smile before she moved towards the door. The Cardinal watched her go and then, as the door closed behind her, he said to the Comte,

"How could you have fathered anything so exquisite? For the first time, Gérard, I think I am rather envious of you."

"She is lovely, is she not?" the Comte remarked, "And very like her mother."

As if knowing that the Cardinal wanted an explanation, he went on,

"Fleur came from Normandy and that, of course, accounts for Syrilla's fair hair and blue eyes. I have always said that she looks more English than French, but I assure you she is very much a Frenchwoman. Moreover she cooks just like one, so don't be afraid that you will not enjoy your dinner."

He paused before he asked eagerly,

"Do you recall that dirty little restaurant we used to patronise on the Left Bank because it was cheap?"

"Of course I remember," the Cardinal answered.

"I have not thought of it again until this moment," the Comte went on, "but how amusing it was on Saturday nights when we used to talk and argue until the early hours."

"And the room was so thick with smoke that one could not see across it," the Cardinal added.

"I think it was those arguments that made me want to write," the Comte commented.

They reminisced for quite some time until the Comte glanced at the clock and suggested,

"I am sure that you would like to wash before dinner."

He paused as if a thought struck him and said,

"Surely you are not travelling alone? Does not a Cardinal, like the Bishop, always have a Chaplain with him?"

"My Chaplain is so often worried about the lusts of the flesh," the Cardinal replied. "As a result he fasts so that he looks as if I ill-treat him, which I assure you I do not! Today is one of his total fast days so he will be content to sit in the carriage or walk about your grounds and will not wish to join us."

"You are sure of that?" the Comte asked. "I would not wish to appear inhospitable."

"And I have no desire that Father Pagerie, who is, I regret to say, somewhat of a bore, should spoil the intimacy of our reunion dinner."

It was in fact a joyous meal.

The food was not only superlative but cooked, as only a Frenchman could appreciate, in a manner that made it taste like ambrosia, while the wine that came from the

Comte's small vineyard was undoubtedly a nectar that would never survive being transported anywhere else.

There was not only good food but also good conversation. The two old friends vied with each other in relating incidents and anecdotes of their past, which made both themselves and Syrilla laugh until the tears came into their eyes.

Syrilla found herself wishing that more of her father's old friends would visit them and entice him away from all his books, which he could seldom be persuaded to leave even for an hour.

Watching her and listening to her the Cardinal thought that she was certainly one of the most attractive and unusual young women he had ever met.

It was not just her beauty that was so striking, it was also, he thought, something spiritual in her face that he did not see in other women, especially those he met in Paris.

If her laughter rang out untrammelled and very occasionally she contributed to their talks a sentence that was witty and gay and it struck exactly the right note.

He realised too that she was not only intelligent but, as might be expected of her father's daughter, extremely well educated.

He made a joke in Latin, which she understood and capped it with a Greek quotation in very much the same manner that her father had done when they had duelled together in words so many years ago.

Finally the Cardinal realised that time was getting on and he knew that he should now give instructions for his carriage to be brought round from the stables to the front door.

And yet he was loath to leave.

This had been an interlude in his busy life which had meant more to him than he could express in words.

It was only as he reached the library that a sudden thought struck him.

"How old is Syrilla ?" he asked the Comte.

"She was eighteen last January," he answered. "I am afraid she leads a very dull life here with me, but as you can see she appears to be content and no man could have a more loving or considerate daughter."

"And yet at eighteen she should certainly be thinking of marriage," the Cardinal said.

The Comte looked uneasy.

"I have, of course, considered it, Xavier, but we live such a secluded existence, Syrilla and I, that I am afraid we receive no invitations and give none. I suppose there are young men in the vicinity, but if there are we do not make their acquaintance."

The Cardinal considered this for a moment.

He knew that if he obeyed his instinct he should say 'goodbye' and leave this little oasis of peace undisturbed and yet he thought that perhaps some Power far greater than himself had guided him here for a special purpose.

How he could conceive such a thing he had no idea, because he knew that what he had to suggest was an outrage against decency or rather against this exquisitely lovely creature who had obviously no knowledge of the world and its wickednesses.

'I cannot do it!' he told himself.

Then he saw the Duchesse's pleading face and was certain that she had not long to live.

How could he return to her, to all intents and purposes empty-handed?

He cleared his throat.

"You have not yet asked me, Gérard," he began, "how I happen to be in Touraine at this very moment."

"I imagine it must be something very important to drag you away from Paris," the Comte replied.

"I consider it to be most important that I should find a bride for the Duc de Savigne," the Cardinal answered.

"Of the Château Savigne?" he enquired. "It is a magnificent piece of architecture? As I expect you know, Xavier, it has great historical significance because in the Middle Ages – "

"I know the history of Savigne well," the Cardinal interrupted.

He knew that once the Comte became involved in historical reminiscences it would be difficult to bring him back to the point.

"What I am going to ask you is whether you would consider a marriage between Syrilla and the Duc."

The Comte stared at him in astonishment and the Cardinal knew that the idea of such a match had never crossed his mind.

"You mean he is the right age?"

"He is a little over thirty," the Cardinal said, "and he bears a great name and owns great possessions."

He paused and then, as if he could find nothing else to say about the Duc, he added,

"Syrilla would make a beautiful Duchesse."

The Comte walked across the library and back before he answered and then he said,

"My wife and I often talked about what we would do when the time came for Syrilla to marry. I have not told you, Xavier, that Fleur was married before. She was a widow and she was in fact thirty-five before we met each other and fell in love at first sight."

There was an unmistakable pain in his voice before he said,

"That is why every year we spent together was so very precious to us both and why when Syrilla was born it was a miracle that we thanked God for."

"I can understand that," the Cardinal said sympathetically.

"Fleur's first marriage was indeed a most unhappy one. She was married when she was very young to a man much older than herself who was a brute and a bully. Because of the way she suffered we swore that we would never submit Syrilla to any arranged marriage."

The Cardinal's spirits dropped.

This was another disappointing answer to his proposition, he thought, and he told himself that he had not been really hopeful even while he had made the suggestion.

The Comte de Monceau, while poor and of no particular social consequence because he was a recluse, was nevertheless the equal in blood and breeding of the Savignes.

It would not be a case of the Duc condescending to marry somebody beneath him if he took Syrilla as his wife.

In fact the situation was, the Cardinal realised, that once again the bride's family was unwilling and he was no further on in finding a wife for the Duc of one of the oldest families in France.

"My wife and I planned that, when the time came, we would ask Syrilla whether or not she was willing to marry the man in question," the Comte was saying. "As you can imagine, Fleur had a horror of a *mariage de convenance*."

"Yes, I can understand that," the Cardinal said, "but, as Syrilla has never met the Duc of Savigne, there is hardly much point in asking you."

And there was no question, he thought, of her being able to meet the Duc.

The Duchesse had told him in her letter that Aristide had refused to meet his bride before he actually married her and by this time he would have gone back to Paris to his disreputable companions and the excess behaviour that made the Cardinal feel sick when he thought about them.

"It is getting late," he said, "and I think, Gérard, I must be on my way."

"No, wait a moment," the Comte exclaimed. "You have made me a proposition and I think it only right and proper that, as it concerns my daughter Syrilla, she should hear what you have to say."

He smiled and there was a mischievous look in his eyes as he went on,

"After all, if nothing else, it will prove good practice for her in refusing the overtures of importunate young men! Now that you have put it into my head, I can see I must try to be a little less selfish and consider her future."

"I certainly think you should do so," the Cardinal said. "You may wish to live in the past, Gérard, but Syrilla has the present to think about. And she is very lovely."

"For once, Xavier, I accept your sermonising and admit I have been in the wrong," the Comte replied. "I shall turn over a new leaf."

"Not of a book, I hope," the Cardinal cried. "That would be fatal for you would forget everything else but what is on the printed page."

They both laughed in the affectionate manner of old friends who had shared many jokes together.

The Comte then went to the door to open it and call for Syrilla.

She came running towards him saying,

"I feel sure that you are going to tell me that His Eminence is ready to leave. I was just making sure that his coachmen and outriders have now been fed. His Chaplain has refused everything, food, drink and even to smile at me!"

She walked into the library as she was speaking and the Cardinal said,

"I cannot believe that there are many men who can do that."

"He looks very miserable," Syrilla said. "Can it be possible that Your Eminence is cruel to him?"

"He is cruel to himself," the Cardinal answered. "I cannot help feeling that to him even laughter is one of the temptations of the Devil."

"I hope not," she said, "because if so we three will all spend a long time in Purgatory!"

She looked so lovely, smiling up at him with her eyes twinkling and the dimples showing on each side of her mouth, that once again the Cardinal had an impulse not to disturb the even tenor of her ways.

But already it was too late.

"His Eminence has put a proposition to me, Syrilla," the Comte was now saying, "which I think you ought to hear."

"What is it, Papa?"

"His Eminence has asked whether you would be prepared to accept the hand in marriage of the Duc de Savigne!"

As the Comte spoke, the Cardinal hoped that Syrilla had never heard of the Duc for he felt he could not bear to see her expression alter and become shocked or disdainful.

Worse still, that he would see in her eyes that disgust which he had felt when he learnt of some of the Duc's more outrageous exploits.

But to his astonishment there was at first an expression of incredulity and then one of radiance mirrored in her eyes.

"The Duc de Savigne ?" she asked in a low voice. "Do you really mean – the Duc?"

"You know he lives not far from here at Château Savigne," the Comte said.

"I know. I went there once with Mama," Syrilla replied.

She looked enquiringly at the Cardinal.

"But – why should he be – interested in me?"

"The Duc wishes to marry," the Cardinal said. "It would make his mother happy and it would make me very happy, Syrilla, if you would consider him for your future husband."

As he spoke, he hoped that God would forgive him, not only for what he was saying but also for even suggesting to this exquisite child that she should become the wife of Aristide de Savigne.

There was a pause and it seemed to the Cardinal that Syrilla's eyes grew larger and more radiant and an inner light seemed to glow from her that he could not understand.

Then, as both men waited, Syrilla said in a low voice that was very clear,

"I would be – honoured – deeply honoured and very – proud to be the wife of the Duc de Savigne."

For a moment it was impossible for the Cardinal to speak. He stared at Syrilla as if he could not have heard her aright.

Then the Comte said,

"Do you mean what you are saying?"

"Yes, Papa."

"But you have never met the Duc."

"I have – seen him," Syrilla answered, "and I have thought of him very often."

The Comte stared at her in perplexity.

Then he said a little uncertainly,

"If that is – what you want – "

It seemed to the Cardinal that he had difficulty in collecting his scattered senses.

"I know it will delight Madame la Duchesse the Duc's mother," he said to Syrilla, "when I tell her of your decision. I am quite certain that tomorrow you will receive a letter from her asking you and your father to visit her at the Château."

He waited for Syrilla or the Comte to say something, but, as neither of them spoke, the Cardinal went on,

"I think I should explain that the Duchesse is in ill-health, in fact it is unlikely that she will live for very long. I therefore suggest that the marriage is not too long delayed. Perhaps it could take place next month in June if it would suit you and, of course – the Duc."

He could not help a little pause before the last words.

He would not put it past Aristide, he now thought, even at the last moment, to evade his responsibilities and refuse to marry the girl his mother had chosen for him.

What was more the Cardinal was quite certain that, if the Duchesse died, there would be no question of marriage, however far advanced the arrangements had already gone.

"I am prepared to do whatever the Duc and his mother think best," Syrilla said.

There was still that almost unnatural radiance in her face that the Cardinal just could not fathom.

He could not credit for one moment that Syrilla, as the daughter of her father and mother, was interested in acquiring an important title.

Yet then one never did know with women. Perhaps the zenith of her ambition was to be a Duchesse.

But even as he thought of it, the Cardinal was sure that it was not true.

No, there was something else, something he did not understand in her quick acceptance of the Duc's offer and the way that the prospect of this marriage seemed to have made her so rapturous.

'But who could feel such a rapture at the thought of marrying the Duc de Savigne?' he asked himself cynically.

Who, but a girl quite ignorant of the Social world, could never have heard of the things that were said about him or the depths of degradation that he had sunk to.

As if he realised that his daughter was finding it hard to speak, the Comte suggested,

"We shall wait until we hear from the Duchesse and I will, of course, discuss this matter further with Syrilla when you have gone to be quite certain that this is really what she wants to do."

The Cardinal felt sure that the Comte had no knowledge himself of the Duc's reputation.

At the same time he could not help suspecting that, because they had been so close in the past and because the Comte was a very perceptive man, he sensed that there was something not straightforward in the offer that the Cardinal had made.

Perhaps he guessed that his heart was not wholly in it.

And yet the die was cast.

There was nothing the Cardinal could do now in the face of Syrilla's acceptance but to carry the news to the Château Savigne, knowing that the Duchesse would rejoice in what he had to tell her.

The only trouble was that he felt a traitor, positively a Judas. to his old friend.

He told himself that he had been certain that, if the Comte had not refused him, Syrilla would, and yet he had achieved what he had set out to do and now wondered why his success should taste like dust and ashes.

'Perhaps she will change her mind,' he tried to comfort himself.

Finally, as he said his 'goodbyes' and the Comte with Syrilla standing beside him waved from the steps of the Château, the Cardinal leant forward to wave in return.

As he did so, he thought that Syrilla in her white gown, her fair hair silhouetted against the Greystone of the Castle, looked almost as if she did not belong to this world.

She might have been a nymph risen straight from the silver water in which the Château was reflected or an angel who had dropped down from the skies to bemuse the mere humans of this world.

But Syrilla and Aristide de Savigne!

The Cardinal shuddered at the thought and like ghouls haunting him he saw the headlines in the newspapers in which the Duc's scandalous exploits were reported by pens dipped deep in vitriol.

He saw a procession of women with whom the Duc's name had been linked, many of whom had cursed him quite openly and many who had suffered both mentally and physically because they had lost their hearts and their minds in his company.

But Syrilla, young, fresh, innocent and as pure as the flowers was to confront a man to whom vice was a constant companion and love an unknown word!

'God forgive me! I have committed a crime for which there can be no forgiveness,' the Cardinal said to himself.

Even his prayers were no solace as he recited them while the carriage rolled on towards Château Savigne.

CHAPTER THREE

As Syrilla approached the bed, the Duchesse Douairière opened her eyes.

For a moment she looked at the vision of white beside her and then, as Syrilla raised her hand to her lips, she asked,

"You are married?"

"Yes, *Belle-mère,* we are married," Syrilla replied softly.

Life seemed to come back into the Duchesse's eyes and the colour to her face.

"I have been praying all night that you will make each other happy," she said. "Where is Aristide?"

"He will be coming to see you later, *Belle-mère,*" Syrilla answered. "Not all the guests have left."

She had refrained from distressing her mother-in-law by telling her that, when she and the Duc had driven back the short distance to the Château from the Chapel in the grounds, he had stepped out first and, as the footmen were assisting her with her full gown and long train, he had walked into the hall and disappeared.

Syrilla could hardly believe her eyes as the guests began to arrive that he would not help her to receive them and she told herself that it must be because he was feeling ill.

It had indeed been very hot in the Chapel, which was filled to overflowing.

The guests in their silks and satins were packed in very closely and the scent of perfume mingling with the heavy fragrance of flowers and incense was overpowering.

Syrilla herself had felt as if she could hardly breathe.

The Brussels lace veil that had been in the Monceau family for generations contributed to this and she had hoped that, when it was raised from her face' she would not look too hot and flushed for the Duc's first glance at her.

But, when the right moment came, she knew that he had not looked in her direction and, driving back to the Château in a fine open carriage, he concentrated on waving languidly to the employees and tenants on his side of the carriage.

Always perceptive where other people's feelings were concerned, Syrilla was well aware from the moment she reached him at the steps of the Chancel that something was perturbing him.

There were vibrations emanating from him that were very different from the excitement and awe which she felt herself as she approached the Sacrament of Marriage.

She had accepted the fact that the Duc found it just impossible to meet her before the Ceremony and the excuse that he was kept in Paris on important affairs seemed to her entirely valid.

Her father indeed was perturbed and more than once the Comte asked her with a worried expression on his face if she was really sure that she wished to be married to the Duc.

"I would have liked to meet him before you actually became his wife," he had said quite reasonably.

"I know Papa, but what I am sure makes it really impossible for him to visit us is that the Wedding, owing to his mother's health, must take place so quickly."

"You have all the rest of your lives together," the Comte complained. "I should have thought a few days delay would not matter."

"The Cardinal has made all the arrangements," Syrilla replied.

She did not wish to argue with her father and, when he continued to discuss the matter, she was silent.

He looked at her curiously, knowing that she had changed in a way that he could not account for.

When he tried to question her about her reasons for wishing to marry the Duc, he found for the first time in their lives that there was a barrier between them and, although he longed for her to confide in him, she did not do so.

He comforted himself with the fact that when she was married she would not be too far away. It only took an hour to reach the Château Savigne from Monceau-sur-Indre.

Yet nothing could console him in his knowledge that he would miss Syrilla desperately, however engrossed he might be with his books.

There was a light in Syrilla's eyes and a smile on her lips that made everyone who knew her think that they had never seen her look lovelier or appear happier.

When she received all the guests in the huge ballroom of the Château, there was hardly a person who did not remark on her beauty.

As the carriages came up the long drive and turned into the courtyard to deposit their colourful occupants in front of the wide sweep of the marble steps of the Château, Pierre de Bethune had come to Syrilla's side.

She was standing in the place appointed, which was banked with roses and lilies and was wondering shyly what she should do as there was still no sign of the Duc.

"I am Monsieur le Duc's Comptroller," Pierre de Bethune explained. "So may I suggest, Madame la Duchesse, that, as I cannot find the Duc for the moment, your father should start receiving the guests at your side?"

"You do not know where Monsieur is now?" Syrilla asked, her blue eyes worried as she raised them to Pierre de Bethune's.

"I think he must be somewhere in the grounds," he said, "and I am sure he will return before long."

"Yes, of course," Syrilla agreed. "It would be kind of you to ask Papa to stand beside me."

Her father then came at once at Pierre de Bethune's invitation and she knew as he took his place beside her that he was extremely surprised at the bridegroom's behaviour.

There was, however, no chance at all of discussing it because the guests, announced by a Major Domo in stentorian tones, began to pour into the ballroom.

There was hardly anyone whom Syrilla had met before and she wished that she could have been greeting instead the servants, the farmers and tenants amongst whom she had many acquaintances and who were being entertained in the great Tythe Barn of the Estate.

After the Reception was over, more than three hundred people sat down to luncheon in the magnificent Banqueting Hall that had been built in Medieval times and was one of the largest in Touraine.

There was still no sign of the Duc and, sitting at the top of the table with an empty chair beside her, Syrilla would have felt embarrassed and a little lost if everybody had not done everything possible to make her feel at ease.

At the same time she felt the meal, as course succeeded course, was far too long.

The food was superlative as might have been expected.

The chefs at the Château had been working for weeks preparing the dishes which were the specialities of the Province.

There was *carpe à la Chambord,* the big ugly carp from one of the many lakes prepared according to a recipe of the chef of King Francois I.

Langue de boeuf en paupiette, stuffed ox tongue rolls, was a favourite from the table of King Henry II, but most of the dishes represented the classic simplicity of country cooking.

As Syrilla expected, there was the popular black pudding of Tours, huge salmon caught in the Loire, jellied chicken livers, which were very popular in Amboise, besides Civet game stews and *gibelotes* and rabbit *fricassées* beloved by those who lived in Bourgueil.

The Vouvray *blanc* or the Bourgueil *rouge*, which came from the Duc's own vineyard, as everybody assured Syrilla, was better than any other that was grown locally and there was no doubt that the guests were all thoroughly enjoying themselves.

Only Syrilla felt that there was indeed something wrong in the bridegroom's absence and she could only hope that in some way that she did not understand she was not the cause of his disappearance.

It was Pierre de Bethune who told her that the Duchesse Douairière wished to see them both as soon as it was possible for them to go to her rooms.

It had been, Syrilla knew, a very bitter disappointment to the Duchesse that she could not actually see her son married.

"I must be well. I *will* be well!" she had said over and over again as soon as the date of the Ceremony had been chosen.

But owing to the heat and the fact that every day she seemed to look a little frailer, the Doctors had been adamant in saying that it would be too much for her.

On her various visits to the Château since her engagement had been announced, Syrilla had learnt how sensitive the Duchesse was about anything that concerned the Duc.

She would not for anything in the world have upset her mother-in-law by relating how strangely he had behaved after the Wedding Ceremony.

"It was kind of you to come and see me," the Duchesse said in her soft voice.

"I would have come long before if I could," Syrilla answered, "but I thought the meal would never end and everybody ate as if they had never seen food before!"

She gave a little laugh and her dimples showed as she added,

"I would not be in the least surprised, *Belle-mère,* if they had not been fasting for a week in anticipation of the feast that they would enjoy here!"

"Has the Cardinal left?" the Duchesse asked her.

"His Eminence was obliged to return to Paris the moment the Ceremony was over. I wish you could have heard his address, it was very sincere and very inspiring."

"I am sure it was."

"And so was the Service."

Syrilla felt as if the Nuptial Mass had brought a special Blessing to her marriage.

Yet, as she was carried away by the great beauty and the solemnity of it, she was still conscious that the man kneeling beside her was somehow unmoved by the whole Service.

She told herself that she was being imaginative and yet she knew she was not mistaken.

"You must go back to your guests, my dearest child," the Duchesse said. "Thank you for coming to see me and tell Aristide to visit me as soon as he can get away."

"Yes – of course – *Belle-mère.*"

Syrilla bent and kissed her mother-in-law's cheek. Then, curtseying, she also kissed her hand before she turned and left the room.

As she went, the Duchesse was praying again that this beautiful girl would bring her son the happiness she so longed for him to find.

Letting herself out of the Duchesse's room, Syrilla walked along the broad corridor that led from the South wing towards the other parts of the building.

She was sure that by now nearly all the guests would have gone and she thought that no one would mind if she went up to her own bedroom to remove the huge tiara of diamonds that she wore heavily on her head.

It was very heavy and had obviously been intended for someone larger and stronger than herself. She would in fact have been far happier if she could have worn a conventional wreath of orange blossoms.

But the Duchesse had told her that it was the tiara that was always worn by the brides of the de Savignes.

As Syrilla wished to do everything that was expected of her, she would not have thought of refusing to follow the family tradition.

She had, however, been quite adamant that she would not wear the other overwhelming jewellery, which were heirlooms, and the necklace of diamonds, each one almost the size of a *centime*, the long ropes of perfect pearls that seemed to hold lights in them, the bracelets, the enormous rings!

She looked down now at the plain gold circle that the Duc had put on her finger and felt that it was all the jewellery she ever wanted and so she would treasure it more than anything else.

She had felt herself tremble when his hands held hers as they made their marriage vows and behind her veil she looked at his face and thought, as she had expected, that he was one of the most handsome and attractive men it was possible to imagine.

The Cardinal had joined them together saying,

"*Ego conjugo vos in Matrimonium, in Nomine
Patris, et Filii, et Spiritus Sancti.*"

Then, having blessed the pieces of gold and silver and the ring, the Cardinal had handed them to the Duc who had placed the ring on Syrilla's finger saying,

"*With this ring I thee wed, this gold and silver I thee give, with my body I thee worship, and with all my worldly goods I thee endow.*"

Syrilla felt herself quiver as he spoke the words in a deep voice and prayed from the very depths of her soul that she might be worthy of him and that he would love her.

Now she told herself that, when the guests had gone, they would be alone and they could talk intimately with each other.

She had reached the centre of the Château and from the top of the stairs she could see through the open door that there were only two or three carriages still left outside.

She was just about to go to her bedroom which was known as *La Chambre de la Reine* as it adjoined *La Chambre du Roi*, where the Duc slept, when she heard voices.

She was passing one of the State Rooms where the guests had left their wraps and she realised that there were two ladies inside and so wondered if it would be polite for her to say 'goodbye' to them.

She was hesitating as to whether to go in or not when she heard one of them say,

"Of course the poor Duc has never been the same since that terrible tragedy. I have heard people say that it changed him completely."

"What happened?" another voice asked.

"You must know about it," the first lady replied, "but no, you were too young at the time. It caused a sensation I can assure you! "

"What was it?"

"The fact that the Duc's *chère amie*, a woman whom many people thought he might even marry, was strangled."

"Strangled? But by whom?"

"By a man called Tonchon."

"For what reason?"

"Jealousy!"

"Who was she?"

"A ballerina by the name of Zivana Mezlanski. She was well known in Paris and making a name for herself on the stage when the Duc fell head-over-heels in love with her."

"With a ballerina? That could hardly have pleased his mother!"

"I believe Zivana Mezlanski was a very exceptional dancer and, of course, the Duc was young and impetuous, only just twenty-one."

"You say that the woman was strangled?"

"It was, of course, a ghastly crime and must have been horrible for him, but they say – "

The speaker's voice then dropped and Syrilla could not hear exactly what she said, but she caught the last words,

" – women mean nothing to him now!"

She had stood listening, hardly aware of what she was doing and, as she turned to go, she heard the older woman adding,

"He has a special Chapel or Shrine to the woman somewhere here in the Château. All her things are preserved there, even her ballet shoes. But no one is allowed to enter it except for himself."

"Are you serious?"

"Completely serious. Everyone talked about it at first. Then, like so many other things, it has been forgotten as the years passed."

"I must say," the younger woman laughed, "the Duc looks as if he has not forgotten and is still in mourning for his lost love. I have never seen an attractive man look more lugubrious at his Wedding!"

"I thought the same," the first lady agreed. "But come along, we must go. I am sure that we are the last to leave."

With a start Syrilla realised that if they left the room at once, they would find her outside the door.

Picking up the front of her skirt, she hurried away down the corridor, moving so swiftly that she was sure that they would not see her.

She entered her own bedroom and closed the door behind her.

She walked to the exquisitely carved dressing table to stare in the gilt mirror supported by cupids and yet she did not see her own reflection.

Now she was beginning to understand, she thought that it should have been so obvious before and that she had been very obtuse.

Why could she not have realised, she wondered, that there was something strange in that the Duc did not wish to see her before the actual Ceremony and that all the arrangements had been made by his mother?

She would have been most unintelligent if she had not realised in the meetings that she had had with the Duchesse how much she longed for her son to be married.

She had shown Syrilla portraits of him at almost every age since he was born and it was easy to understand that what the Duchesse yearned for more than anything else was that her only son should have children, especially a son.

Again and again she told Syrilla that the Château was too big for only one child.

"I often thought that Aristide was a very lonely little boy," she said wistfully. "His father and I did our best. We had children to stay, we invited local boys to have lessons with him, but it was never the same as having brothers and sisters of his own."

"No, of course not," Syrilla had agreed.

"Perhaps it has – made him a little – reserved," the Duchesse said hesitatingly. "Perhaps he is not as effusive and – extrovert as many other Frenchmen."

Syrilla had not paid a great deal of attention to this at the time.

She had, of course, enjoyed seeing the portraits of the man who was to be her husband and she had been deeply touched when the Duchesse had given her one.

But she had her own ideas of what the Duc would be like and what he would feel and yet now –

She felt uncertain and unsure of herself and the rapture that the Cardinal had sensed in her and which had been with her ever since she had learnt that she was to marry the Duc was overshadowed.

*

The Duc walked into the Château by one of the windows opening out into the garden and saw with satisfaction that the guests had all now left.

He was aware that the servants would be tidying the ballroom and the Banqueting Hall and so he proceeded to another wing where there was a great library in which his father had always sat.

It was furnished not only with books but also with some of the finest chests and tables in the house.

The sofas and chairs were deep and comfortable and, as the Duc threw himself down on one, he thought with satisfaction that tomorrow he could return to Paris.

He was married and he hoped almost savagely that his mother was now fully satisfied.

When he left the Château, having agreed to accept the marriage she desired, he felt as he rode back to the City that he had been trapped.

He did not believe, despite her frail appearance, that his mother was as ill as she wished him to think and, when the Cardinal visited him in his Paris Mansion, he suspected who it was he had to thank for the position that he now found himself in.

"Your future bride is very beautiful, my dear boy," the Cardinal told him.

The Duc's lips had twisted disdainfully.

He was certain that his idea of a beautiful woman and the Cardinal's were very different. Besides Paris was full of beautiful women and nowhere were there more of them to be found than in his own house.

There was, however, only one thing that he was curious about.

"Why, Your Eminence," he asked, "did you choose a de Monceau as my future wife? I should have thought that a daughter of the Duc de Foucauld-Fleury would have been more suitable. Their blood is already linked with ours some centuries ago."

"The Duc's only unmarried daughter is already affianced," the Cardinal replied.

"Indeed! Then let me see, who else is there in this benighted Province? God knows there are enough famous houses cheek by jowl from which you could have taken your choice."

The contempt in the Duc's voice stung the Cardinal into telling the truth.

"The Viscomte de Boulancourt's daughter's engagement was announced in the papers a week before I called on them and the Marquis d'Urville informed me categorically that he would rather see his daughter dead than let her become your wife!"

If His Eminence had hoped to shock the Duc, he was mistaken.

The Duc merely flung back his head and laughed and it seemed for just a moment that he forgot his languor and his cynical indifference.

"Good for d'Urville!" he exclaimed. "At least he is truthful. I imagine that the Comte de Monceau feels the same except that a Dukedom was too appetising a bait to be refused."

"On the contrary," the Cardinal said, "neither my friend, the Comte de Monceau, nor his daughter know anything of your reputation."

The Duc looked sceptical and the Cardinal said,

"That is the truth, I assure you. The Comte is a recluse and his daughter is completely innocent of the world outside the small village where they live."

"How very delightful!" the Duc sneered. "A bovine wench who thinks only of the soil and doubtless smells like it!"

For one moment the blood rushed to the Cardinal's head and he felt a very un-Christian desire to strike the sneer from the Duc's lips.

Then a wise instinct that had always stood him in good stead told him to say no more.

Let the Duc find out for himself just what Syrilla was like.

'A bovine wench indeed! He would soon discover that he was mistaken!

*

The Duc realised, having missed his midday meal, that he was both hungry and thirsty.

He rose to tug at the bell-pull and then settled himself once again in the armchair.

A servant came into the room and looked surprised at seeing him.

"You rang, *Monsieur le Duc*?"

"I want something to eat and a bottle of our best wine."

The man hurried away to obey his order and the Duc, looking around the room, recalled a time many years ago when his father had been sitting at the desk and his mother on the sofa.

He heard his own voice telling them about a girl he had met in Paris.

"She is so beautiful, Mama! *Exquisite*! And, although she is a ballerina, she is in fact the daughter of a Russian Nobleman."

"Then why is she on the stage?" his father asked without turning round.

"As she has such an exceptional talent, her parents allowed her to train with the Imperial Russian Ballet. As you know, dancers in Russia have a different status from what they have in this country."

"Is she very beautiful?" his mother had asked.

"I want you to see her, Mama. May I bring her home when she can get away from the theatre? They are rehearsing for a new ballet, but I might be able to persuade her to come to the country for Saturday night and perhaps Sunday."

There was only the slightest hesitation before the Duchesse replied,

"But, of course, Aristide dearest, your friends are always welcome here."

He had a feeling at the time that there would be an argument later between his father and mother over the invitation, but, as he had achieved what he wanted, he kissed his mother and went from the library into the garden.

Every flower, every movement of the leaves blowing in the breeze had made him think of Zivana.

Never had he thought that it was possible for any woman to move so exquisitely or have an allurement that seemed at times to make her enchanted.

'She has captured not only my heart but also my imagination,' he told himself.

Nothing could be a better setting for her beauty than the great Château that had belonged to his ancestors and the twin lakes reflecting the spires, the turrets and the statues on its roof.

"God, but I am happy!" he exclaimed as Zivana and his home seemed indivisibly linked in his mind and he thought that no man had ever been more fortunate.

His memories were interrupted by the servants bringing in large trays of food, setting the dishes down on a side table. But now the Duc decided that he was no longer hungry.

"Pour out the wine," he said, "and inform Madame la Duchesse that I wish to see her."

The servant bowed in acknowledgement of the command and the Duc drank down the glass of wine in two gulps.

He was thinking that the sooner he fulfilled the duty that was required of him the quicker he could return to the life that he was familiar with and which he had deliberately chosen.

He realised that he had no idea what his bride looked like. His mother had told him when he arrived the previous evening that there was a portrait of her given to him by the Comte among the Wedding presents, but he had not been interested enough to look for it.

'What did it matter what she was like?' he asked himself and after tonight he could leave her.

There had only been one woman who had really mattered in his life, and she –

His lips tightened and there was darkness in his expression as he drank deeply.

The ghosts from the past etched the lines under his eyes more deeply than they had been before and the cynical disdain on his face made him appear almost sinister.

He rose and, as he did so, saw himself reflected in a mirror on the other side of the room.

Mockingly he raised his glass.

"Here's to posterity!" he jeered, "and a future Duc to carry on the historic name I have embellished so nobly!"

His glass was still raised when he heard the door open behind him.

For a moment he did not turn and when he did so he thought he must be mistaken and this was not the wife he expected but a young girl who was little more than a child.

She stood there looking at him and he stared incredulously at the fair hair that was like sunlight against the book-lined walls, the blue eyes and the translucent purity of her skin.

For a moment they held each other's eyes. Then impulsively, as if she was eager to reach his side, Syrilla moved towards him.

The Duc was too much a connoisseur of women not to notice the grace of her slender body and the way her small head was poised on a long neck.

She swept to the ground in a deep curtsey and as she rose she said,

"Monseigneur! I have wanted so much to talk to you."

The Duc stared at her.

"What – did you call me?"

A faint flush rose in Syrilla's cheeks as she answered,

"*Monseig – neur.*"

"That is the title usually reserved for dignitaries of the Church or Princes of the Royal blood."

"I am aware of that – but it is the – way I have – always thought of you."

"Always?" he questioned.

"Ever since I first saw you."

The Duc raised his eyebrows.

"I do not recall any meeting."

Syrilla laughed.

"You are hardly likely to. I said that I had seen you and that is the truth, but you were not likely to notice me amongst a crowd of a thousand – no perhaps two thousand – others."

The Duc gestured with a hand towards the sofa.

"Suppose you sit down and tell me about it?" he suggested.

Syrilla did as he asked and the Duc leant back in the armchair he had recently vacated.

His eyes were on Syrilla's face.

'The Cardinal was indeed right,' he thought, 'she is most certainly unusually beautiful, but God knows what I have in common with a child of that age.'

Not that it was of any importance since he was returning to Paris tomorrow.

"What were you going to tell me?" he prompted as Syrilla was silent.

"I was thinking that you look exactly as you did nine years ago – no – that is not true. You look sad, which you did not then – and that I – do understand."

"I do not follow you," the Duc said. "Tell me where you first saw me?"

"I should have thought that you might have guessed," Syrilla said. "At the tournament that was given here in the Château grounds on your twenty-first birthday."

"But of course!" he exclaimed, "I had forgotten about it. My father and mother revived the jousts that had taken place in Medieval times."

"And you were the Knight – the White Knight," Syrilla said softly.

There was an expression in her eyes that told the Duc, as did the note in her voice, that she had been moved by his appearance in the shining armour that had belonged to one of his ancestors.

The jousting had been skilfully arranged and meticulously rehearsed.

The Black Knight, his opponent, had gained two minor victories, then he had challenged him and, of course, because it was all play-acting, won when good triumphed over evil.

He could remember now the cheers and applause that had gone up from the stands and the crowd that had come from far and near throughout the Province of Touraine to be present at such an auspicious occasion.

The crowd had been jolly, noisy and good-humoured, filled with beer and cider, which his father dispensed very liberally, whilst in the stands all the beautiful young women from the adjacent Château had been attired in Medieval costume.

The Duc recalled carrying the favour of some lady who presented it to him formally, but he had thought romantically as he fought that the favour which mattered most was Zivana's miniature, which he carried in a locket around his neck.

Perhaps, as he was fighting for someone he loved, it had made him appear very dashing and certainly as romantic as everyone wished him to be.

"Nine years ago," he said reflectively.

"I was nine too," Syrilla added, "and I have never forgotten how you looked – and you – inspired everyone who saw you."

"It was only a performance."

There was silence for a moment.

And then Syrilla said,

"May I tell you – something, *Monseigneur,* now that we are – alone?"

"Yes, of course," he replied. "There has not been any chance of having any conversation until now."

"I did not understand – I did not know until a little while ago – what you felt."

The Duc looked puzzled.

He could hardly imagine that his mother had actually told this child what his intentions were towards his wife and their future together.

He had, however, made them quite clear to his mother last night when she had talked as if he intended to stay at the Château for some length of time.

"I have obeyed your wishes, Mama," he announced in a hard voice. "I am giving up my freedom because you have asked it of me and I will therefore endeavour to see that you have the grandchild you yearn for so ardently. But that is all!"

He paused to add firmly,

"We made a bargain, you and I, and I will fulfil my part of it."

"What do you mean, Aristide?" the Duchesse had asked.

"I mean that I intend to go back to Paris and to live there."

"For – ever?" the Duchesse faltered.

"For as long as it suits me," the Duc replied. "My wife can stay here and you can keep her company, but I do *not* intend that she shall in any way interfere with me any more than I shall interfere with her."

"But – Aristide! – " the Duchesse cried.

"There is no point in discussing it, Mama," the Duc interrupted. "Nothing you can say and nothing you can do, will make me change my mind. One night should be enough to make sure that your fondest hopes are realised and then you will have no further hold over me."

He knew as he spoke that he was being brutal. At the same time he was fighting to free himself from the soft silken chains by which the Duchesse had endeavoured to hold onto him once before and failed.

There was a long silence and the Duc knew that his mother was fighting against the tears which threatened to overwhelm her.

He walked towards the door.

"Goodnight, Mama," he had said and left before she could say anything more.

Now, he told himself, he would have to make his position very clear to his wife and he wondered how and with what words he should begin.

Because he found it difficult, he said almost sharply,

"Tell me what you wish to say."

Syrilla's eyes were very large in her pointed face.

Then unexpectedly she moved from the sofa to kneel down at the Duc's side.

"I did not realise," she said in a soft voice, "until now what you had suffered ten years ago."

The Duc stiffened.

"Who told you?"

"I overheard two ladies talking after I left your mother's room," she replied. "The elder one was saying how deeply you had – loved and how – tragically you had lost that love. Oh, *Monseigneur* – I now understand!"

"What do you understand?"

"That you have only married because it would therefore please your mother, that you had dedicated yourself to an ideal and only for your mother's sake have you fulfilled her wishes."

The Duc did not speak and, after a moment, Syrilla went on,

"I have always known that everything you did and thought would be noble and this great love is what I might have expected of you."

The Duc was now staring at her incredulously, but with her eyes looking up into his she continued,

"It is the pure selfless love of the Troubadours, who dedicated themselves, as you have done, to serve the lady they worshipped until they died."

Syrilla made a little gesture with her hands.

"Now I have learnt what happened," she said in a low voice, "I promise that I will not be any trouble, that I will help you so that no one will ever know."

"Know what?"

"Just as your love is too sacred to be talked about by outsiders," she answered, "so the arrangement between us will be a secret. Although I am your wife in – name, I will respect the – path you have chosen and I shall intrude as – little as possible."

Perhaps for the first time in his life the Duc found himself bewildered to the point when he could find no words to express himself with.

The admiration, which was almost adulation in Syrilla's eyes, did not escape him nor did the awed note in her voice, which made it seem as if she spoke of something very sacred.

How, he asked himself, could he explain to this child that he was not dedicated to any great ideal and that what had happened in the past had turned him into the cynic he now was?

With an effort he found his voice and asked,

"Are you telling me that you think I should not actually make you my wife?"

"I know you might do so out of duty to your mother," Syrilla replied, "but I know too it would go against your deepest – instinct and you would feel even if you – kissed me that you – betrayed the love that is in your heart."

She looked away from him a little shyly as she said,

"The lady I was listening to said that you had a special Shrine or Chapel here in this house where you had locked away all the things that belonged to the woman you loved. I can understand that your heart is in there too."

She paused for a moment before she went on,

"The lady also said that women mean nothing to you now. So, as I am a woman, even though legally I am your wife, I can mean nothing and that I will – accept."

She looked at him again as she added,

"I do not believe that any other man could be so wonderful or so noble and, having loved you ever since I was a little girl, I love and reverence you now more than I could express in words."

The Duc felt almost as if he was in a dream.

How, he now asked himself, could he possibly explain that she had misinterpreted what she had overheard?

Women meant nothing to him!

He almost laughed thinking of the hundreds of women who had passed through his hands so many in fact that in many cases he could not remember either their faces or their names.

But how could he say this to his wife now kneeling at his feet, looking up at him with an adoration she would give to a Saint.

Never, he thought, with all the women he had known, had there been one who looked at him in just that sort of way and, while it was a new experience, at the same time it made him feel uncomfortable.

With difficulty he tried to find words to explain to Syrilla that she had been mistaken.

"You saw me as the White Knight when you were the age of nine and I was twenty-one," he said. "I am now thirty and I have changed and altered considerably in the past years."

A smile illuminated Syrilla's face.

"Of course," she answered. "Papa says that anyone who does not grow wiser every year, every month, every minute, is a fool. We are sent into the world to learn and, of course, as we develop we know more and I think that we should feel more."

She made a little gesture as if she was afraid that the Duc would misunderstand her.

"I can guess what you must have felt when you suffered such a tragedy. It must have torn you in pieces, but I think now you will be even more resolved in your dedication than you were then."

Her voice softened as she carried on,

"And yet you are prepared to sacrifice everything that you hold dear for the sake of your mother. That was very very wonderful of you, but it is what I would have expected."

The Duc felt that he was becoming mesmerised by what she was saying.

"I must explain, Syrilla," he said hastily, "and you must not have such romantic notions about me. I am, after all, human and certainly not like the Knightly figure I may have seemed in armour."

Syrilla then rose to her feet and suddenly the Duc saw the dimples on either side of her mouth.

"Now you are going to disparage yourself and decry your own greatness, *Monseigneur*," she said, "but I am not going to listen and, please, although I know that you are thinking of me – you are not to do so. I am content, utterly and completely content to be your wife and to admire you because you are everything a man and a gentleman should be."

She did not wait for an answer but moved across the library to stand for the moment in one of the windows.

The sunlight illuminated her hair and the Duc thought for a moment that she had a halo round her head, before she said with a lilt in her voice,

"There are so many things we can do together here. I want to visit your vineyards, I want you to tell me about the treasures there are in this house, for I am sure every one of them has a history and I want very much to see you catch a fish in the lake."

Again the dimples were in her cheeks as she added,

"You don't know what a temptation those lakes are to your neighbours. Quite a number of the gentlemen told me today that they are often tempted, because you are so seldom here, to poach the fat trout that lie among the reeds."

She laughed as she went on,

"And one of your neighbours has just threatened that if you don't do something about the deer, which are far too numerous, he will hunt them himself."

'I must explain to her that I am leaving for Paris tomorrow morning,' the Duc thought, but somehow the words would not come to his lips.

He rose to his feet and, as he did so, Syrilla moved across the room towards him.

She slipped her hand into his with the confiding gesture of a child.

"Do you think there will be time before dinner for us to go and explore the garden?" she asked. "I have wanted to do that so much every time I have come here, but then I thought it would be more fun for us to go together."

She paused.

"I long to see where you played when you were a little boy and most of all I want to see where I first saw you, on the ground that was used for the jousting."

The Duc told himself it was only right that he should make an effort to please her after the way he had behaved during the Wedding.

"I am sure we have time," he said, "and after all dinner can wait until we are ready for it."

Syrilla's eyes twinkled at him.

"What will the chefs say if we spoil their souffles?"

"Let them spoil!" the Duc replied.

CHAPTER FOUR

With a little difficulty Syrilla drew her horse to a standstill and looked back to cry over her shoulder,

"I won! I won, *Monseigneur*!"

The Duc drew even with her, thinking he had never seen any woman who sat on a horse better or, despite her fragile appearance, had such good sure hands.

They had raced in the Park over the ground where the joust had taken place and where Syrilla had seen him as the Knight in Shining Armour.

He had known as soon as he saw her mounted on one of his finely bred animals with an Arab strain that she was an exceptional horsewoman.

At the same time with the stallion he was riding he could have beaten her in the race with comparative ease.

On an impulse, which he did not understand himself, the Duc had allowed Syrilla to reach their chosen goal first.

It was something he had never thought of doing in past years, having always in every way, even down to the smallest detail, wished to dominate whatever woman he was with.

"You rode well," he said as he drew his horse up alongside her.

She looked up at him and said,

"I have a fancy, *Monseigneur*, that once again you have been chivalrous."

"You are too perceptive, or perhaps I should say, too intelligent, Syrilla."

"I am sure you would not wish your wife to be anything else," she replied. "You are so clever yourself that I am afraid of boring you with my stupidity."

"How do you know I am clever?" he asked, feeling curious to hear her answer.

"Your mother has shown me all the prizes you took at school and at University."

"Book learning, repeated parrot-wise!" the Duc said disparagingly.

"You don't expect me to believe that," Syrilla answered. "Papa always says that it is not what one reads that matters, but the way in which new horizons are opened up in the mind."

"I have long ago given up looking for horizons – "

"That is not true," Syrilla interrupted him, "and, if you think me intelligent, it is because I believed deep within myself that I should one day be able to talk to you just as we are doing now."

It was extraordinary, the Duc was to think later in the day, that he could in fact talk with Syrilla as he had never talked with another woman.

With other women the conversation, if there had been any, had always centred around the woman herself and her attraction for him.

Every word had a double meaning, every phrase was an enticement not of the mind but of the body.

With Syrilla it was very different.

She asked him innumerable questions because she was interested and curious, but she also contributed what she herself thought and felt and the Duc found himself stimulated in a way that he had not been stimulated for a long time.

He sensed that much of what Syrilla said derived from all that she had learnt from her father.

At the same time there was always her original ideas and the way in which she appeared to look at things from quite a different angle from what he might have expected.

"How can you know so much about the Orient," he asked during one argument, "when from what you have told me you have never travelled?"

Syrilla's eyes twinkled at him.

"People can go round and round the world and see nothing but their own backyards," she answered. "I would love to see the places we have been talking about. At the same time, because I have studied them, I almost feel as if I have been there and they are so real to me."

"Most girls of your age would be thinking about men, not books and ruins of the past."

"I was always in fact thinking of one man," she answered, "and striving to make myself worthy of him."

The Duc's expression was sceptical.

"There must have been other men in your life besides one mythical Knight whom you might never meet."

"Of course there were men," Syrilla answered. 'There was the *Curé* who, when I wore a new bonnet in Church, always averted his eyes. I think that he thought I was one of the temptations of St. Anthony!"

There were dimples on both sides of her mouth as she went on,

"Then there was Farmer Bastie's son. He once brought me half a pig to show me his affection, but he blushed so red when he gave it to me that it was difficult to know which was the pig and which was the man!"

The Duc laughed as if he could not help it.

"You know perfectly well, Syrilla, that I am talking about Beaux. In the great Châteaux near your home there must be innumerable ardent young Noblemen who, I am quite certain, scoured the country in the hope of finding someone who looks like you."

"In Monceau-sur-Indre I must have been invisible," Syrilla answered, "and I was very happy to be with Papa and think of you."

"Quite frankly, I don't believe this obsession that you had for a man you had seen only once," the Duc said mockingly. "You are straining my credulity, Syrilla, even though it is extremely flattering to think that one look at me when you were hardly out of the nursery has meant so much to you all these years."

"It is true. *Monseigneur*," Syrilla said with a note of sincerity in her voice that could not have been assumed. "And remember that, although I only saw you one day, when Mama and I came to the Château there were pictures of you in many of the books in Papa's library."

He raised his eyebrows and she explained,

"They may have been entitled *St. George, Sir Galahad, Jason Searching for the Golden Fleece* or *Odysseus,* who had himself lashed to the mast when passing by the island of the Sirens. But whoever the pictures depicted, to me they were always you."

Her eyes lit up as she went on,

"I used to tell myself stories in which you killed the dragon and did innumerable deeds of heroism and valour."

The Duc did not speak and after a moment she said,

"But no, I think I should have imagined you as a Troubadour singing,

"If Heaven be gained by love and prayer,
Then I at once should enter there."

The Duc made a little sound that might have been one of exasperation and Syrilla said quickly,

"Forgive me. Perhaps you think it is an impertinence of me to speak of your true love. I will not do it again."

The Duc rose from the chair beside Syrilla after they had finished dinner to walk across the room to look at the last dying rays of the sun sinking behind the high trees.

"Nothing we could say to each other should be an impertinence, Syrilla," he said after a moment, "and I think it important that we speak frankly and that is why I want – "

He paused because he was searching for words to express what he was trying to say, but before he could find them, Syrilla had sprung from the sofa to move across the room to stand beside him.

"That is what I hoped you would say, *Monseigneur*. I have always talked openly to Papa, saying anything that might come into my mind and so I would hate that there should be any barriers between us. I love you and there is nothing I can give you but my thoughts."

The Duc wanted to say that she could give him much more but then, looking into the innocence of her blue eyes, he found it impossible.

Almost abruptly he changed the conversation.

"Tell me why you walk so gracefully," he asked. "You must have had a lot of lessons in deportment and dancing."

Syrilla laughed.

"The only teachers of those sort of accomplishments in Monceau-sur-Indre are the birds or perhaps the fawns in the wood."

"Are you telling me that you have not been taught to dance?" the Duc enquired.

To his surprise there came an anxious expression to Syrilla's face as she replied,

"I was so hoping you would not ask me that."

"Why?"

"Because, *Monseigneur*, I have never danced – with a man, I mean."

"You have never been to a ball?" the Duc asked incredulously.

"After Mama died there was no one to take me, even if I had been asked to one," Syrilla explained. "And Papa would have hated having to put on his 'best bib and tucker' and sit on a dais with the Dowagers."

She smiled and then again there was an anxious expression on her face as she said,

"I would not wish you to be – ashamed of my ignorance in any way. Perhaps we could find a teacher so that, when I am really proficient, I could attend a ball with you."

"There is no hurry for that," the Duc replied automatically.

"I know you do not have time for such frivolities," Syrilla said, "and I was going to ask you, *Monseigneur*, whether I could possibly help you in any way with your work in Paris."

"My work?" the Duc questioned in surprise.

"Yes, *Belle-mère* told me about it."

"Indeed. And what did she say?"

"I asked her what you did and she told me, 'my son is concerned with the people of Paris who are unfortunate'."

The Duc smiled at his mother's evasion of the truth. And yet she had managed to provide her daughter-in-law with an answer to an awkward question.

"I have heard so much about the poverty and misery," Syrilla went on, "that exists in the slums and how the people are often starving, besides being wounded and perhaps killed by the rioting."

"I believe that is true," the Duc admitted.

He was thinking that he had never concerned himself with such matters except to hope that his own property should not be damaged by the Revolutionaries.

"That is just what I would expect you to do, to help such people," Syrilla said. "Perhaps, if it was no trouble, I could come with you to Paris sometimes and see your work for myself."

The Duc had a sudden vision of her at one of his outrageous parties. He knew only too clearly how women like Susanne, Aimie and Rosette would shock and bewilder her.

"I have no wish for you to come to Paris," he said sharply.

"I would not desire to do anything you would not want me to do," Syrilla replied. "At the same time, *Monseigneur*, even the most Holy of men do not scorn the help of their disciples."

She smiled a little tremulously as she added,

"I am a very willing disciple – as you well know."

"We were speaking about dancing," the Duc said, "not the sordid conditions of Paris. If you do not learn to dance and never go to any of the parties to which you will undoubtedly be invited in your position as my wife, what will be the use of all those extremely pretty gowns that you have in your trousseau?"

Syrilla then looked down at her gown, which was made of pink gauze with the full skirts draped and ornamented with rose-buds and pale blue ribbons.

"I have never owned such beautiful dresses before," she said. "Did you know that your mother gave them to me as a present?"

"I had no idea," the Duc replied.

"*Belle-mère* was so very kind. She realised that living so quietly with Papa I hardly knew what the fashions were, so

~98~

she sent my measurements to Paris, described what I looked like, and all these elegant and exciting gowns arrived. I was so touched by her generosity."

The Duc guessed that his mother's generosity lay in the fact that she wished Syrilla to attract him. There was no doubt that the gowns, which showed the whiteness of her shoulders and accentuated the tininess of her waist, made her look very lovely.

But there was something more than mere beauty about her, he thought, that made her different from other women he had known.

It was that she was so intensely alive and that when she was animated she seemed almost to sparkle as she spoke, while her eyes shone as if they had captured the sunlight.

"I must tell *Belle-mère* that you have admired my gowns," Syrilla enthused. "And – *Monseigneur* – will you forgive me if I say something very – personal?"

"I thought we had already agreed to be frank with each other," the Duc replied.

"Then will you tell your mother just how much you – love her and how much she means to you?" Syrilla asked. "You are her whole life. She thinks and dreams and prays for you and I think that every word you have ever said to her is carved on her heart."

The Duc did not reply and after a moment Syrilla went on,

"She is so happy that you are married. I think, if you had refused to do as she asked, she would have died feeling that she had nothing left to live for."

"Did she tell you that?" the Duc asked sharply.

"No, of course not," Syrilla answered, "but I knew it instinctively when she talked to me about you and when I saw the happiness in her eyes when I went to her room in my Wedding gown."

"I should have gone there with you," the Duc commented unexpectedly.

"I understand now why you disappeared," Syrilla replied, "but you must never let your mother suspect for one moment that we are not behaving like – like an – ordinary bride and bridegroom."

"You know she wants me to have an heir?" the Duc asked slowly.

Syrilla nodded and he continued,

"Is it right for us to deny her something that she desires so fervently?"

He waited for Syrilla's answer, feeling surprisingly tense.

"I have – thought about that," she said, "and I do realise that it is important for you one day to have an – heir to inherit your – title and your vast possessions."

"And what is your solution?" the Duc quizzed her.

"I thought – and please do not think it presumptuous of me – perhaps one day, when we have known each other longer, you might look upon me as a friend – and feel that as a friend I could – give you a child."

The words were spoken softly and then, before the Duc could reply, Syrilla went on,

"I know it will be difficult for you to think of me in such a way and I am not quite – sure – how a man and a woman – make love so that they have – a baby."

There was a little pause before she continued,

"But, although you cannot ever – love me or give me your heart – it would be wonderful – very very wonderful for me to have your – child."

The Duc took a step forward. Then, before he could touch Syrilla, she said,

"I am only speaking of something that may happen in the – future. It may be years before you feel you can – touch me in such a way – and I would not like you to think that I am not conscious of your goodness or the sacred dedication of your vow of chastity."

She did not understand the expression on the Duc's face and she said quickly,

"P-please forgive me that I – spoke of this again, but you did – ask me and once again I am telling you my thoughts."

"And I am listening to you with great interest, Syrilla."

This was the opportunity, the Duc told himself, when he should make things very clear to her.

But somehow like quicksilver the moment evaded him and he found himself talking of other matters and unable to direct the conversation back into the channels he wanted.

Later, however, when he went to his own room he was determined there should be no more shilly-shallying.

He would make it clear to Syrilla once and for all that he was her husband and intended to behave as such.

He next thought how much he would laugh at another man if he was told how the poetic dreams of a young girl prevented him from making love to her and so treating her as a man should treat the woman who was his wife.

A number of bawdy anecdotes concerning impotent husbands came to his mind and he decided that he would have no more nonsense and, what was more, the sooner he returned to Paris the better!

As his valets helped him to undress, his own thoughts mocked and jeered at him. He told himself that he must be growing senile if, after being the lover of every woman who took his fancy, he could not explain to a girl of eighteen what he wanted of her.

'It is simply because she is so unsophisticated that I find it so difficult,' he thought, 'but doubtless she is like every other woman, acting a part, and by no means as innocent as she appears.'

Yet while he scoffed at his own hesitation he knew that no woman, however brilliant an actress, could produce the expression of great adoration in her eyes that Syrilla had when she looked at him or force such a note of sincerity into her voice.

'The whole concept of me as a Knight in Shining Armour is absurd!' the Duc asserted to himself when his valets left him alone. 'God knows, if any of my friends heard Syrilla talking in such a manner, they would laugh their heads off.'

He knew his reputation better than his critics. He was well aware of the results of every outrageous exploit and he read the newspaper reports of his behaviour with amusement.

He had deliberately set out to defy the conventions, to shock decent men and women, to become a byword for everything that was debauched and immoral.

He had succeeded, but strangely enough it had not eased the hurt that had caused him to behave in such a manner and the wound within himself had not healed.

"Curse it, but I am becoming morbid!" the Duc called out aloud.

He looked around the great room with its carved panels, its painted ceiling and the huge, canopied velvet bed with the Royal Coat of Arms embellished above the headboard.

Suddenly he felt furiously angry.

"It is this damned house!" he cursed. "It is the ghosts of my ancestors peering over my shoulder! I will go back to the sewers of Paris where I belong and where I feel the most at home."

It was as if he defied and challenged his forefathers.

Yet he felt as if they were reaching out to him from the grave, striving to draw him back into their circle and under their influence.

They were all calling out to him. He could almost hear their voices and see the pity and condemnation in their eyes.

'I will not listen to you!' he wanted to shout. 'I have escaped you once and I will escape again!'

He picked up a candle from the bedside table and the movement made the flame flicker and the grease ran down over the gold candlestick and from there to the carpet.

Turning, the Duc pulled open the communicating door that connected *la Chambre du Roi* with *la Chambre de la Reine*.

Between the two rooms there was a passage in which there were wardrobes, a powder closet and also a bathroom for the use of the Duc. The one attached to *la Chambre de la Reine* was on the other side of the Suite.

He moved along the passage, his feet making no sound on the thick carpet.

He was wearing a velvet robe and his feet were encased in velvet slippers embroidered with his insignia.

It was many years since he had opened the door into *la Chambre de la Reine,* in fact, not since he had been a child and his mother and father had then used these rooms.

In the morning he would run happily up and down the passageways between them, first to nibble at his mother's breakfast and then to watch his father being shaved by his valet.

His mother's room had always smelt fragrant from the flowers that stood in big bowls on gilded tables whatever the time of year and the perfume she had used had a very distinctive scent all of its own.

It seemed to the Duc that he smelt now the fragrance of the flowers, but the perfume was different.

It was one that he had noticed on Syrilla earlier in the evening and it reminded him of spring flowers. He thought in fact that it was jasmine, one of the first heralds of spring.

He realised that he had been sitting in his own room for so long that it must be quite late.

As his hand went out towards Syrilla's door, he suspected that she might be asleep and he did not wish to frighten her.

He turned the handle very gently and, as the door opened, he looked into the room.

But Syrilla was not asleep and one glance at the huge bed draped in silk, the pale azure blue of *Sèvres* china, showed him that it was empty.

Then, by the light of the candles burning on either side, he saw that Syrilla was kneeling on the *Prie-Dieu,* the prayer stool that stood facing the wall opposite the bed.

It had been there in his mother's time, but he had never actually seen her praying on it.

Syrilla was kneeling there now, in only her nightgown with the lights from the candles picking out the gold in her hair.

The fingers of her hands were pressed tight together like a child's and, although she was kneeling upright, her head was bowed and her eyes were closed.

The Duc stood looking at her, then suddenly she raised her head and looked at the picture above the *Prie-Dieu.*

The Duc knew it well.

It was one that one of his ancestors had brought home from Florence, a copy of a picture by Botticelli called *The Magnificat.*

It had been his favourite picture as a child. The Madonna held the baby boy on her lap, surrounded by angels, who held a crown over her head.

It was then that the Duc realised that Syrilla's beauty had the same spirituality that could be seen in the faces of the angels painted by Botticelli.

Quite unaware that he was watching her, she had a radiance in her face that was not of this world.

He knew without being told for whom she prayed and what she asked for in her prayers.

Then, as if her purity created an invisible barrier between them that he dared not pass, he closed the door quietly and went back to his own bedroom.

*

The Duc was breakfasting in the sunshine in the small oval-shaped room that was kept exclusively for the first meal of the day.

He had just helped himself liberally to a dish of *fritures,* small fried fish from the Loire, when Syrilla came into the room.

"Please – don't move, *Monseigneur,*" she begged as the Duc began to rise from his chair. "I am early, but it is such a lovely day and I am so longing to ride with you as you promised we should do – to the vineyards."

"I had not forgotten," the Duc replied. "In fact I have sent a message an hour ago to tell my Manager to expect us. I am sure that he will want us to sample the different vintages we have in the wine caves, so you must be careful not to fall off your horse on the way home!"

"I don't think I should drink very much," Syrilla said seriously.

"I will prevent you from doing that," the Duc replied.

She smiled at him in a way that made him think that any man would be only too anxious to take care of her.

"You have had breakfast?" he asked.

"Yes, thank you," she replied, "but not such a substantial meal as yours. Dare I steal one of your *croissants*? And I never thought of asking for honey. I am sure that the honey from your bees is better than from anyone else's in the whole of Touraine."

She did not wait for his permission and spread a *croissant* with butter and honey.

"If I listened to you, I should become conceited not only about myself but also about my possessions," the Duc said in an amused voice.

"And why not?" she asked. "They are better than anyone else's! Why, only yesterday I heard your Head Groom saying that there was not a horse between here and Nice to equal the one you were riding."

The Duc laughed.

"And doubtless my herdsman thinks that my cows give better milk and my cattle better beef than any other animal between here and Cherbourg!"

"I am sure they are right," Syrilla said quite seriously. "And the guests at the Wedding kept exclaiming how delicious your wines are."

The Duc finished what he was eating and said,

"I cannot remember having such a large appetite for years. I suspect that the air here also is better than anywhere else."

He was teasing Syrilla.

At the same time he knew quite well it was not the inferior air of Paris that prevented him from having an appetite in the morning, but the amount he drank the night before and the excesses that he indulged in.

Now he felt unexpectedly most athletic and healthy as he followed Syrilla across the hall where he was handed his hat, his riding whip and his gloves.

Their horses were waiting for them outside and he thought that Syrilla's riding habit of white pique, which was the latest fashion in Paris, was even more becoming to her than the pale green one which she had worn the day before.

The groom helped her into the saddle and the Duc was just about to mount his stallion, which was resisting the efforts of two of his grooms to hold him steady and bucking in the most obstreperous manner, when Pierre de Bethune came running down the steps.

"There is a letter from Paris, *monsieur,* which needs your immediate attention," he said to the Duc.

"Immediate?" the Duc questioned.

"It is said to be of the utmost urgency and the groom is waiting to carry your reply back to Monsieur Layfette."

This was the name of the Duc's lawyer and, if Pierre said the matter was one of urgency, then it must be.

He looked at Syrilla whose horse was already fidgeting to be off and said,

"Ride on slowly. I will catch you up."

She smiled at him and cried,

"Please do not keep Monseigneur long, Monsieur de Bethune. We have so much to see before luncheon."

"I will be as quick as I can, *madame*," Pierre promised.

There was a look of admiration in his eyes that was unmistakable as he spoke. Then he hurried after the Duc, who was already striding impatiently back up the steps into the house.

"What is it?" he asked as Pierre joined him, and they walked side by side towards his office which was a short way down one of the corridors.

"It is trouble, I am afraid, *monsieur*."

"What sort of trouble?" the Duc asked curtly.

Pierre de Bethune handed him a letter that had come from his lawyer and he read it with a frown on his face.

A woman, one of the more disreputable of the many *cocottes* whom he had entertained and who for a very short while had captured his fancy, had been arrested.

The Police had found in her possession a number of articles that she had taken from the different men she had slept with, some of which were very valuable.

From the Duc she had stolen an emerald ring bearing his monogram, several gold items equally easily identifiable and some sapphire and diamond cufflinks.

What the lawyer had related in his letter to the Duc was that the Police wished him and every other man from whom the woman had stolen to support a charge against her.

This would mean her receiving a long term of imprisonment, but it would also result in their names being mentioned in Court.

The Duc read the letter through slowly.

Then he said,

"I don't mind losing the jewellery, but then the gold ornaments are a valuable part of the family collection. They were in fact given to one of my ancestors by Charlemagne. I dislike the thought of losing them."

"Do you not think it possible, *monsieur,* for the Police to return them to you without your bringing a case against the woman?"

"She will tell the Police that I have given them to her. Those women always make some excuse," the Duc answered.

"Then you will prosecute?"

The Duc hesitated.

He did not know why, but he had a sudden dislike of letting all Paris know that he had been associated with a woman who was not only a *cocotte* but also a petty thief.

She had her attractions, he was not denying that, but it seemed to him particularly sordid that, while he had been asleep, she had taken the cufflinks from his discarded shirt.

He thought for a moment.

Then he said sharply,

"I will not prosecute. Notify all jewellers and those creatures who sell stolen goods that I am prepared to buy back any pieces that carry the Savigne Coat of Arms."

"I hoped you would say that, *monsieur.*"

The Duc raised his eyebrows.

"Why, Pierre?"

Just for a moment he thought that his Comptroller would not tell him the truth, but then almost defiantly Pierre de Bethune said,

"Madame la Duchesse might hear of it and it would hurt her."

There was silence and Pierre wondered if the Duc would rebuke him for speaking the truth, as he had done so often before.

But to his surprise the Duc merely said quietly,

"Yes, Pierre, it would hurt her."

He turned to hurry after Syrilla, but outside the Comptroller's office he found his Agent waiting for him.

The man had a list of complaints from tenants who considered their rents were too high in relation to the repairs that their landlord did for them.

It took the Duc some time to extricate himself and, when finally he mounted the stallion, which was now behaving even more skittishly, Syrilla was out of sight.

*

Syrilla had not meant to go quite so far from the Château, but the horse she was riding was fresh and wished to gallop.

When she looked back, she realised that she could no longer see the great house.

She had ridden to the very edge of the Park and so in front of her there were now thick woods. She thought that the cutting through them, which she and the Duc would take to the vineyards lay to the left.

However she had no intention of going any further without the Duc and she turned back to look for him. But, as she did so, from the shelter of the trees a number of men appeared.

She looked at them in surprise, seeing that they were ordinary labourers, but all of them carried long sticks in their hands and one or two even held ancient pikes.

To her astonishment they surrounded her horse and one man put his hand on the bridle.

"Who are you – what do you want?" Syrilla asked.

"Where's the Duc?" a man demanded.

He was an uncouth-looking individual with long hair hanging almost to his shoulders and he wore clothes that were tattered and torn.

The others were of similar appearance and the expressions on their faces as they looked at her made Syrilla feel uneasy.

There had been no sign in Monceau-sur-Indre two years ago of the Revolution, but that had not prevented Syrilla reading descriptions of what had taken place in some other parts of the country.

She knew that in Paris two thousand soldiers and people had been killed and over five thousand wounded.

There had been many casualties in every town in France and desperate fighting, as she had learnt from her mother's relations in Calvados and Normandy.

The man who had his hand on her bridle started to pull the horse forward into the wood.

"What are you doing?" Syrilla demanded.

"You're comin' with us," the man answered.

"You cannot take me away," Syrilla cried. "This, as you must well know, will do you no good. If you have something to say to the Duc, come to the Château and ask him to listen to you."

"And get whipped or shot down for our pains?" the man asked jeeringly. "We meant to take the Duc this mornin', but likely enough you'll do as well. After all 'tis only right that the new Duchesse should see how her people live."

He spoke in a way that was singularly unpleasant and Syrilla thought that it would be a mistake to bandy words with him.

The other men were muttering to themselves and they all looked so rough and unpleasant that she knew that there was nothing she could do but let them take her where they wished.

Even if the Duc should find her now she was afraid for him, the stout sticks and the pikes that the men carried would prove effective weapons against a man who carried nothing but a riding whip.

Quite suddenly the crimes perpetrated by the Revolutionaries swept into her mind to start her heart beating faster.

It was not only heads that had tumbled into baskets under the guillotine thirty-nine years ago. There had been innumerable instances since of aristocrats living in the country being set upon and even killed by peasants and in some cases their wives and children had been shown no mercy.

Although her lips were by now dry, she held her chin high and tried not to hear the rude comments of some of the men and the coarse jokes they made to each other as they walked along behind her.

They emerged onto the other side of the wood and now Syrilla had a view of the Duc's vineyards stretching away for what appeared to be miles.

The vines were in leaf and the bunches of grapes, although still small and green, were easily discernible giving evidence that there would be a good harvest this year.

On reaching the vineyards the men surrounding her turned right and moved away from the broad acres down the side of the wood.

After some time they came to a valley that was hidden by trees and which had a small insignificant stream running through it.

They had been moving at a quick rate for over half-an-hour when Syrilla saw ahead what appeared to be a small village.

There were vines growing around it and then as they grew nearer she saw that the vines were different in appearance from those that they had passed earlier on.

There were no leaves on the brown roots, no buds and no young shoots.

"Are you lookin' round you?" the man asked savagely. "You come from this part of the world, I believes, and you knows what a vine should look like when you sees one."

"I can see these are dead – or dying," Syrilla answered. "What has happened?"

The man let out a loud and ugly laugh.

"Her asks what's happened!" he said to the other men. "Shall we tell her? Perhaps she'd like to drink the wine that comes from 'em!"

He spoke in a jeering voice and with a violence that made Syrilla want to shrink away from him.

"I can see there is a disease," she said. "Surely the vines should have been uprooted and burnt."

She spoke seriously, but her words were greeted by jeers and catcalls.

"If the Duchesse knows what should be done, why don't she tell the Duc and get him to give an order?"

There was a burst of voices in answer to this and in the medley of sound Syrilla realised that this was what they had wanted the Duc to see and this in fact was their grievance.

She wondered why the diseased vines had been left, but felt that it would not be safe to say too much without having a real knowledge of what had happened.

Further on they reached the little village and now she could see the dilapidated condition of some of the houses.

From a distance they had seemed quite attractive, but now she could see gaping holes in the roofs, windows hung with sacking and doors hanging askew on their hinges.

A number of children came into the roadway to watch them ride by and one look at them told Syrilla what was wrong.

These people were starving!

Their faces were grey and lined, the children's cheekbones stood out and their arms too seemed to have no flesh on them.

They moved very slowly past the houses and Syrilla had the feeling that the women in the doorways were too apathetic even to jeer at her or to shout as the men had done.

They had moved on a little further when an elderly woman came running from one of the houses holding something in her arms.

The man leading Syrilla's horse by the bridle stopped and the woman ran to the tall man who had spoken to her first and had been walking at her side.

She thrust out what she held in her arms towards him and, looking down, Syrilla saw it was a baby – a very small baby with a wrinkled face and closed eyes, which must have just been born.

"Dead!" the woman shrieked. "*Dead!* And what do you expect with its mother without a bite to eat?"

The man stared for a moment at the dead child and then looked up at Syrilla.

"This is your doin'," he said. "*Damn you and damn all aristocrats!* You've killed my son and you deserve to die!"

He almost spat the words out at her, but Syrilla was not listening. She was looking at the baby and something stirred in her memory.

Without waiting for anybody to help her, she slipped down from her horse and, going to the woman, took the child in her arms.

She touched its face gently with her fingers and realised that it was still warm, although certainly it looked dead.

Then she bent her head and did what she had seen Jacques do to the lamb.

She drew in her breath and blew as hard and as violently as she could through the baby's half-open lips.

Again she blew, giving her breath to the child.

Surprised into silence by her action, nobody moved or made any attempt to stop her.

Then, as she breathed into the baby's mouth another time, one of its little hands stirred and a second later it gave a faint cry.

It was hardly audible and yet those standing nearby heard it.

"It's a miracle!"

It was the woman who had brought the child from the cottage who whispered the words.

Then she gave a shrill shriek.

"The baby's alive! He's alive! It's a miracle! God be praised! *It's a miracle.*"

The child cried again and Syrilla drew the rough blanket in which he was wrapped closer and handed him back to the woman.

"Take him to his mother," she then told him. "Tell her to keep him warm and feed him as soon as possible."

The woman gasped as if she had no words in which to reply. Then as she moved away Syrilla realised that everybody was staring at her incredulously.

For a moment it seemed as if they were all turned to stone.

Then the women crossed themselves.

"That was my son!" the tall man beside Syrilla said unnecessarily.

"I think he will live," Syrilla said quietly. "Now, suppose you tell me what is wrong and why the vines have died."

CHAPTER FIVE

Everybody talked at once and for a moment through the mêlée of sound Syrilla found it difficult to make sense of anything that was said.

Then she heard one word '*pyrale*' and understood what had happened.

Her father had told her often about the menace that different moths were to the vines. He had explained to her about the *cochylis* or night moth, which was first found in Champagne in 1771.

The *cochylis* strings threads of silk between the flowers and buds and late in the summer a second generation settles on the grapes, pricks them and causes them to turn mouldy.

There was also the *vex blanc du Hanneton* or the white moth of the Cockchafer, which is a particular enemy of the young vine and the grafted cuttings, besides the red cochenille moth which lays its eggs in June and its larvae a month later,

All these were feared and dreaded by the wine-growers, but then the *pyrale,* a large moth whose body is yellow, with yellow wings, was perhaps feared most of all.

The Comte had told Syrilla that caterpillars hibernate in the bark of the branches all the winter to emerge in the spring. After spinning webs over the vine they proceed to devour the buds, the young shoots and the leaves.

Syrilla had listened and remembered what he had said. However they had been fortunate at Monceau-sur-Indre and each year the grapes had ripened without any mishap, making the Comte delighted with the wine that he was producing.

Now she realised that she was seeing for herself the terrible devastation that the *pyrale* moth could inflict on a vineyard.

She knew only too well that there was nothing that could be done about it and the only remedy was for all the vines to be dug up, the stumps removed with as many of the roots as would yield to pressure.

When a vine has been in the ground for twenty-five years, its roots are embedded in the soil and enormous strength is required to uproot the stump.

This meant, Syrilla knew, scooping out a great hole round the dead vine with pickaxes and crowbars and then hauling out the stump with a chain harnessed to a horse.

This was usually done as soon as the disease showed and Syrilla could not understand why in this vineyard the vines had just been left and the men not ordered to remove them.

When she could make her voice heard, she had asked what the Duc's Manager had done about the disease when they had reported it to him.

"He told us to find work elsewhere," an elderly man answered.

"And was that impossible?" Syrilla enquired.

"Who wants us at this time of the year?" several of the men replied almost in unison. "In the harvest, yes, but we've been paid no money since the beginnin' of April."

Now Syrilla understood why they looked so ragged and why they seemed to be suffering from starvation.

They explained graphically how at first they had their vegetables to eat while the men from the village searched far and wide over the countryside for other jobs.

Then in desperation, as the children were hungry, they killed their goats and chickens, which meant that they had no milk or eggs.

Growing still more desperate they decided when they heard about the Duc's marriage that they must take violent action to acquaint him with their plight.

Syrilla gathered that it was the tall man whose son's life she had saved who had thought of kidnapping the Duc to make him fully aware of their problems.

They knew, she learnt that, when he was at the Château, he rode every morning in the Park and they decided to take him forcibly to their village to see the conditions for himself.

What they had not expected was to find Syrilla riding alone and she had the feeling that while she was their hostage they were a little embarrassed because she was a woman and not the man they wanted.

"The Duc'll come to look for you," one man said gruffly, "he'll not want to lose his new wife so quickly."

There was some laughter at this, but it was not the jeering rudeness that Syrilla had heard when the men had brought her from the Park to their village.

Now they were looking at her not only with respect but with something like awe and she knew that the women thought she had performed a miracle that had also had an effect on their husbands.

While she was talking to the men who were now in a circle around her, the women and children had congregated on the outside.

Many of the children had sores and abrasions on their faces and hands and Syrilla knew that this sprang from malnutrition.

Now she could fully understand the reason for their appearance.

There had been no money to buy thread, to mend torn clothes, and no money even for a nail to repair the broken shutters over the windows or to mend the hinges on the doors.

There was water in the stream, but she had the feeling that, as their supply of food grew less, the women became far too weak to wash their clothes and pale faces and the lack-lustre expression in their eyes confirmed this.

Finally, when she had heard all that the men had to tell her, Syrilla said,

"It is not necessary for me to tell you that the Duc had no idea that this was happening on his estate. I am absolutely certain it was not on his instructions that you

~122~

were not paid your wages until you could find other employment."

Nobody spoke for the moment and she went on,

"I will return to the Château and ask Monsieur le Duc to come here and see for himself what you are suffering. I know that he will take steps immediately to put everything right."

She made, as she spoke, to walk towards her horse, but the tall man barred her way.

"You'll not leave us," he said. "How do we know that the Duc'll not punish us for havin' taken you away? He might send his servants or even soldiers to turn us out of our houses as his Agent has threatened to do."

He spoke truculently and once again Syrilla felt a little tremor of fear as she saw that his words brought back expressions of ferocity and sullenness to the other men's faces.

With an effort she managed to smile at him.

"Very well," she replied. "I will wait here with you while one of you will take a letter to Monsieur le Duc to explain what has happened to me. Will you please bring me paper and ink?"

This apparently involved some difficulty and, while they were being found, the women drew nearer, staring at Syrilla wide-eyed while one or two of them reached out tentatively to touch the skirt of her habit.

Then, as she smiled at them, they grew bolder and asked her help with their children.

Syrilla was sure there was little wrong except the lack of food, but she knew that until they had money there was no point in prescribing salves or lotions.

Instead she talked with them, telling them what she thought was a good diet for children provided that fresh vegetables and fruit were available and also the eggs and goats' cheese which was, she knew, an essential on a peasant's table in Touraine.

When writing paper and an inkpot containing very pale ink was brought and a quill-pen, which one of the men sharpened, she sat down in the chair they provided for her and wrote at a rough deal table which was badly in need of a scrub.

When she had written her note and folded it, she said to the men,

"I think, to save some time, one of you who can ride well, and I mean well, should take my horse to the Château."

"They'll accuse us of stealin' it," was the answer.

"In which case ride as far as the wood," Syrilla said. "Tie the horse securely to a tree and walk the last part of the journey. When Monsieur le Duc has received the note, the messenger can escort him back here."

The tall man looked doubtful.

"How do we know he'll come alone?" he asked. "If he brings men with firearms against us, we'll fight and you might get hurt."

"Monsieur le Duc will come alone because I have asked him to do so," Syrilla answered.

She knew that they were sceptical. At the same time there seemed to be no alternative to what she had suggested.

Three of the men claimed they were experienced riders and Syrilla chose the youngest of them. He was also the lightest and she had noticed him patting and making a fuss of her horse while she was writing the letter.

He mounted and then he rode off in silence and Syrilla knew, although the men sounded blustering and brave when they talked to her, that they were in fact extremely apprehensive at what would be the result of their action in kidnapping her.

To put them at their ease she sat down in the shade of a tree that grew in the centre of the village and began to talk with the women.

Soon they were seated around her and many of them with their children in their arms.

Syrilla talked to them about her own childhood in Monceau-sur-Indre. She told them that her mother had died and how much she missed her.

She related too how she had first seen the Duc at the Tournament that had taken place at the Château when he was twenty-one.

Many of the women could remember the Tournament and they nodded agreement when she described what a magnificent spectacle it was. Syrilla learnt that the old Duc had given every worker on the estate a week's extra wages to celebrate his son's coming-of-age.

"Any of you who saw Monsieur le Duc then when he was dressed as a Knight will know well that he would always champion the cause of justice," she said, "and that is why when he learns how you have suffered, you need no longer be afraid that he will not right what is so obviously wrong."

*

The Duc, after searching vainly for Syrilla in the Park, had returned to the Château to see if she had come back by a different route and he had somehow missed seeing her.

"She is not here, *monsieur*," Pierre de Bethune told him.

"Then where can she be?" the Duc asked. "I just cannot believe that she would go to the vineyards without me. In fact I rode through the woods and some way into the fields, but there was no sign of her."

"You could not have missed Madame in her white riding habit," Pierre de Bethune said.

The two men were standing on the steps of the Château and all the time he was talking the Duc's eyes had been searching the green Park and expecting at any moment to see Syrilla come riding from between the trees.

"It seems extraordinary," Pierre de Bethune said. "You don't think there could have been an accident or the horse has bolted?"

"I have never known a woman who could ride as well as Madame," the Duc interposed, "and, if the horse had thrown her, I cannot help feeling that he would have returned to the stables."

"Yes, that is true," Pierre de Bethune agreed.

It was then that the Duc noticed a man tramping through the great wrought-iron gates which stood at the entrance to the Courtyard.

He looked at him indifferently. Then, as the man advanced towards the front door and did not turn off to the back quarters as might have been expected, he waited feeling in some strange way that this man was concerned with Syrilla.

As the man drew nearer to where the Duc was standing, Pierre de Bethune realised that he carried a note in his hand.

There was silence until the young man, thin and ragged, reached the foot of the steps and looked up at the two gentlemen towering above him.

"Which of you be the Duc de Savigne?" he asked.

The Duc took a step down towards him.

"I am!" he answered sharply.

"Then this be for you," the man replied.

He thrust out the note as he spoke and the Duc took it from him.

He read it and Pierre de Bethune, watching him closely, saw his lips tighten ominously.

"Where is Madame la Duchesse now?" he asked harshly.

"She be with us at Tauxise," the man replied.

"What is it? What has happened?" Pierre de Bethune asked hastily unable to control his anxiety.

The Duc handed him Syrilla's note and he read,

"*Monseigneur,*

The people who tend one of your vineyards have been harshly and, I feel, unjustly treated since the vines were devastated by the pyrale moth. They intended to bring you here to see for yourself what they are suffering. They have taken me instead.

I have promised them that, as soon as you receive this letter, you will come alone and put things right. The bearer of this note will show you the way.

I remain, Monseigneur,

Your affectionate and admiring wife,

Syrilla."

"They are holding Madame as hostage!" Pierre de Bethune said hoarsely in a low voice.

The Duc turned to look at him and, as their eyes met, they both knew without words what the other feared.

The Duc snapped his fingers towards the groom who was standing holding the stallion that he had been riding until he returned to the Château.

The man moved forward.

"You must not go unaccompanied, *monsieur,*" Pierre de Bethune said in a low voice, "it might be dangerous!"

"You have read Madame's note," the Duc replied. "She has asked me to come alone."

"She may have been forced to write it," Pierre de Bethune suggested.

"That is a possibility," the Duc agreed at once. "Nevertheless I have no alternative but to obey her request."

"Let me send someone with you," Pierre de Bethune suggested, "or for God's sake at least go armed."

"I have a strong feeling that Madame trusts me to carry out her wishes exactly as she has expressed them," the Duc replied quietly.

"Monsieur, listen to me – " Pierre de Bethune begged, but already the Duc had swung himself into the saddle.

"Have I to wait for you, young man?" he asked the bearer of the note.

"I've a horse, Monsieur le Duc. I left it at the edge of the Park."

"Then run ahead and collect it," the Duc commanded.

The man started to run from the courtyard back into the Park and the Duc held his horse as he said to his Comptroller,

"Send for the Manager of the vineyard and have him here to await our return. I want an explanation of this and it had better be a good one!"

"Monsieur, let me go with you," Pierre de Bethune pleaded.

The Duc looked down at him from the height that his position in the saddle gave him.

"Madame wishes me to go alone, Pierre," he said. "I have a feeling that she is visualising me in the role of a White Knight, in which case I shall need no help in slaying the dragon!"

There was a single note of light-hearted amusement in his voice, which surprised Pierre de Bethune and, as the Duc rode away, he stared after him in perplexity.

*

Syrilla had almost exhausted her fund of stories and was in fact finding the hours she had been talking had made her throat very dry.

But she told herself that she had no right to complain when she knew that many of the children, now that the excitement of her appearance was over, were whimpering with hunger.

She had also noticed that the men, sitting around and apparently keeping guard over her, were chewing pieces of wood as if the mere fact of having something in their mouths was a little compensation for the emptiness of their stomachs.

All the time she was talking she had been glancing towards the end of the village at the woods. She had been escorted along the side of them by the men who had brought her here.

She knew it was the way that the Duc would come and when, finally she saw two horses silhouetted against the green trees, she felt her heart give a leap of excitement.

She had known that he would not fail her.

Yet at the same time she had been half-afraid that because people were so apprehensive of anything that appertained to a Revolution, he might, despite her request, have brought a number of his grooms with him.

But there was no mistaking the Duc's upright figure on his great black stallion and she felt as if her love went out towards him in a great wave of warmth and adoration.

As Syrilla watched the Duc approach the village, so did everybody else.

He was riding fast and, now that he had been shown by his guide where Tauxise lay, he appeared to spur his horse forward and come towards them at a tremendous speed.

Slowly the men rose to their feet and the women and children did likewise. As the Duc reached the houses, Syrilla moved swiftly towards him.

It seemed to her that he had eyes for no one else and he swung himself from the saddle taking her outstretched hands in his and raising them one after another to his lips.

"You are all right?" he asked urgently.

"You have come! I knew you would come!" she cried.

"You asked me to come alone."

"I am very grateful. You are desperately needed here."

"What is wrong?"

Syrilla made a little gesture towards the vineyards.

"You can see for yourself."

"What is it?" the Duc asked.

"The *pyrale* moth!"

At Syrilla's words the men who had been speechless and at the Duc's appearance found their voices.

"Yes, *pyrale* moth!" the tall man said. "It's not our fault it's killed the vines, but because of it we've been left to starve! Starve, *monsieur*! Look at our women, look at our children, look at us."

The Duc looked round as he was asked to do.

"You have received no wages?" he enquired.

There was a roar of voices at this, all telling him how long they had been without money, how they had been forced to wander over the countryside in search of jobs that did not exist and how they had returned to the village merely because there was nowhere else to go.

The voices rose to a note of violence as the men explained their grievances and the way that they had been treated, but even so the Duc could hear Syrilla's voice as she said softly,

"The children are starving. I managed to save one of them from dying, but others will die unless something is done and quickly!"

The Duc held up his hand for silence and surprisingly he was instantly obeyed.

"I have listened to your complaints," he said, "and I agree that they are entirely justified. I will now give my orders to the men of Tauxise and I expect them to be carried out."

It seemed to Syrilla that everybody held their breath as the Duc continued,

"You will now pull up the vines immediately, clear the land and plant, as is usual in such circumstances, potatoes and mustard. This work should take some months, but you are well aware that these vineyards will have to remain free of vines for the next five years."

The Duc looked around at the men who were listening to him carefully.

"I intend to discover during the next month or so whether it is best to remove this village completely and build you new houses on another part of my estate or whether it might not be reasonable to clear part of the woodland to the West and plant a new vineyard there."

He pointed as he spoke and went on,

"If the soil is good and the position gets the sun, I see no reason why the territory served by the village of Tauxise should not be extended."

There was a little gasp as the Duc's words percolated the men's minds.

"We'd prefer that, *monsieur*," the tall man said after a moment. "Most of us have lived here all our lives."

"We shall, of course, have to go into the problem thoroughly," he said, "and so I would appreciate your opinions as to whether the planting of such a vineyard is really worthwhile."

There was a little murmur at this, but it was a warm one of approval and very different from the mutterings that Syrilla had heard before.

The Duc, looking at the women listening on the outside of the circle, said,

"I do appreciate it as does my wife, Madame la Duchesse, that something has to be done at once for the women and children, in fact for all of you. Your wages will be paid at once and you will be fully compensated for the months when you have received nothing.

"I intend to return to the Château now and I will order that goats and chickens are to be provided for the village from my farm. There will also be grain and flour from my granaries so that you can start baking again."

This time the women cheered and, because it was so spontaneous and at the same time so weak, Syrilla felt the tears come into her eyes.

The Duc drew a purse from his pocket and said,

"I am afraid that I carry little gold with me, but this should be enough to purchase a few commodities from the next village until I send you everything that I have promised. I shall not delay. It will be here this afternoon."

They cheered again and the Duc added,

"I think now it is time that I took my wife home."

The men parted to let the Duc and Syrilla walk to their horses, but many of the women went down on their knees to kiss the hem of her skirt as she passed them.

Only as they reached the horses did the elderly woman who had brought out what she had thought was a dead baby on Syrilla's arrival at the village, come running from a house.

The baby was in her arms and he was crying loudly and angrily,

"Bless him, *madame*," she said to Syrilla. "Bless the child you gave life to. You are an angel come from God Himself!"

As she spoke, the woman knelt down on the dusty road and held up the crying child.

For a moment Syrilla hesitated and then gently she put her hand on the baby's head.

"This child has already been blessed by God," she said. "It is not I who gave him life, but God because life comes only from Him."

Everyone was listening and Syrilla still with her hand on the baby's head continued,

"May I suggest now that you name this child after the man who has helped you and who I know will bring you good fortune for the future?"

She smiled at the Duc as she spoke and added quietly but clearly,

"The name is Aristide!"

"It would be a very great honour, *monsieur*," the father said.

"Then I am delighted that your son should be named after me," the Duc replied.

He picked up Syrilla in his arms as he spoke and lifted her into the saddle. Then, as he mounted his own horse, he said to the villagers,

"The quicker we return the quicker you shall have the things I have promised you."

He turned his horse as he spoke and Syrilla followed him. For a little way the women ran beside her touching her skirt and calling out their thanks. Then at the end of the village they dropped behind and Syrilla waved to them until she and the Duc had reached the woods.

They rode for a little until the Duc asked,

"You were not frightened?"

"Only at first," Syrilla confessed. "But, after I had saved the baby's life, I knew that they would not hurt me."

"Tell me how you did it."

She told him how she had seen her father's shepherd saving the lamb's life and how the Cardinal had said that life came from God, but sometimes it could be transmitted to others.

"I have never heard of anything so extraordinary!" the Duc exclaimed.

'They meant to kidnap you and then threaten you," Syrilla told him in a low voice, "but I explained that you could not have been aware of what was happening to them."

The Duc was silent for a moment and then he said,

"Nevertheless you blame me for letting such things occur on my estate."

Syrilla did not answer.

"Tell me the truth," the Duc insisted mockingly.

She had the feeling that he was almost forcing her to blame him.

"I understand, *Monseigneur*," she said at length, "how you have dedicated yourself to helping the poor and the unfortunate of Paris, but you are needed here too and these are your people."

The Duc opened his lips as if he would reply. Then he spurred his horse on a little faster and there was a look on his face that she did not understand.

When they arrived back at the Château, Pierre de Bethune was waiting for them.

He ran down the steps with an expression of intense relief on his face.

"You are all right, *madame*?" he enquired.

"Quite all right," Syrilla answered, "but Monsieur has a great many things that he wishes to be done at once."

She paused and continued,

"Please hurry with them – it is urgent – very urgent!"

She knew that Pierre de Bethune would obey her request and she walked into the house leaving the Duc giving sharp staccato orders that she had the impression astonished not only his Comptroller but also his servants.

She felt a little tired as she went upstairs to her room. The maids helped her change from her riding habit into a thin gown and she went downstairs knowing that she was very hungry but feeling somehow ashamed when she thought of how the villagers must have suffered at being so long with little or no food.

The Duc was waiting for her in the salon and, when she entered the room, he put a glass of wine into her hand.

"Drink this," he said. "I feel you need it."

"I am very thirsty," Syrilla admitted.

Then, as if she could not prevent herself from asking the question, she enquired,

"Has everything gone for the village?"

"Not everything," the Duc answered. "It will take time to take the goats and chickens there, but to bridge the delay I have already sent Tauxise a considerable amount of food such as hams, fish and bread from our own larders."

Thank you – *thank you*, I knew you would do something like that!" Syrilla cried.

She thought that the Duc was looking at her with an odd expression in his eyes and after a moment she asked,

"Have you seen the Manager of the vineyards?"

"He is waiting for me," the Duc replied. "It will do him good to cool his heels. By now he must know what has happened."

"You intend to dismiss him?"

The Duc paused for a moment before he said,

"I am now wondering if he has sinned more against these people than I have. As you so rightly said, Syrilla, they are my responsibility."

"He was inhuman," Syrilla said, "and that is something you could never be to anyone."

She thought that the Duc was about to say something, but at that moment luncheon was announced and he waited for her to lead the way into the dining room.

Despite Syrilla's protests the Duc insisted after their meal that she should lie down.

"If you are not tired, you should be," he said. "You have been through an experience that would be trying and indeed intimidating to anyone."

"I want to be – with you," Syrilla protested.

"I am going to interview my Manager and Agent," the Duc said. "I have a suspicion that this meeting will not be a pleasant one and quite frankly I would prefer you not to be there."

"Then I will go and lie down," Syrilla agreed, "but please, *Monseigneur,* may we go to the vineyards tomorrow? I was so looking forward to seeing them when I was with you."

"Then we will visit them tomorrow," the Duc promised.

He saw the light in her eyes and told himself that it would be useless for him to think of returning to Paris at the moment when there was so much to be done here on his estates.

'Why,' he then asked savagely, 'could they not have been administered as competently as they had been in my father's time?'

Even as he asked the question, he knew the answer and was afraid to express it even to himself.

*

Syrilla lay down in the beautiful bedroom that had been occupied over the centuries by many Queens of France.

She loved the blue brocade panelling and the painted ceiling depicting Venus surrounded by cupids in soft pinks and blues that were echoed in the *Aubusson* carpet on the floor.

There was a faint breeze billowing the silk curtains and she felt almost as if it brought the sound of music to her ears.

'I am happy,' she told herself, 'far happier than I imagined it possible to be and it is all because of Monseigneur. He is *so* wonderful!'

She thought of what had happened that morning and added,

'It is only because he has been away in Paris that things have gone wrong at Savigne.'

She said a little prayer that the Duc would find so much to do here in his own home and on his own lands that he would not wish to return to Paris too soon.

'They will miss him,' she told herself, 'but he is needed here, desperately needed.'

She knew that it was not only the villagers of Tauxise and other places who needed the Duc. There was a strong yearning within her that they should be together in the peace and tranquillity of Touraine.

Syrilla was afraid of Paris and she thought of how lost, inexperienced and ignorant she would appear in the sophisticated brilliant Society in which the Duc undoubtedly moved and of which she had no knowledge whatsoever.

Had her mother been alive, she thought, she would not have been so afraid, but her father had never been concerned with Society and she was certain that there were a hundred pitfalls and a thousand mistakes she would make unknowingly with no one to guide her.

'Please God,' she prayed. 'Let Monseigneur wish to stay here where we are so happy and it is so beautiful – and there is no one to come between us.'

She did not know really what she meant by her last words and yet instinctively she knew that her contentment was menaced in some strange and unaccountable way.

She had no idea what it might be, perhaps the Duc's preoccupation with the work that he had dedicated himself to and perhaps the people in the village.

She could not formulate any constructive idea of what might be waiting in the future.

She only knew that it was like a cloud looming on the horizon and that it was definitely there, even though the Duc had not spoken again of leaving the Château.

'I love him! Oh, God, I love him with every thought and every breath I draw,' Syrilla prayed. 'Make him love me a little. Make him want to be with me and I will not ask for any more.'

She prayed intensely. At the same time she was in fact a little tired and after a time she fell asleep.

She awoke because her maids came in with her bath and she realised to her surprise that it was time to dress for dinner.

Glancing at the clock Syrilla felt that she had wasted several precious hours in sleeping when she might have been with the Duc.

He would have finished his interviews with the Manager and the Agent and perhaps they could have walked together in the garden or sat on the terrace and she could have talked to him as she loved to do.

"Quickly, quickly, Marie!" she said to her maid. "Bring me my prettiest gown! Then I will go downstairs. Monsieur le Duc always changes early and I want to be with him."

Nevertheless it took a little time to bathe in the rose-scented water and to be dressed in one of the beautiful gowns which the Duchesse had ordered for her from Paris.

It was such a pretty dress of white tulle trimmed with blue ribbons and little posies of pink rosebuds.

As her maid fastened it at the back, she hoped that the Duc would admire her in it. She knew that always when she appeared she searched his eyes for just a glint of admiration that she was sure was sometimes there.

There was a cluster of small pink roses to wear at the back of her head and she clasped around her neck a diamond chain that had been one of her Wedding presents.

From it hung a locket in the shape of a heart and Syrilla decided that when she knew the Duc a little better she would beg him to have a miniature painted of him so that she could wear it in the locket which would always be close to her.

Finally she was ready and, thanking her maid, she hurried from the room onto the wide landing off which led the Grand Staircase that ended in the marble hall.

Because she was in such a hurry to be with the Duc, Syrilla ran down the staircase and seemed almost to fly across the hall towards the salon where she felt he would be waiting.

As the footman opened the door and she passed into it, she saw with a sudden feeling of disappointment that the salon was empty.

Then she realised that the Duc was outside on the terrace and so she moved across the carpet towards the open window.

She had almost reached it when she heard footsteps outside and saw Pierre de Bethune approach the Duc, who was standing against the balustrade looking out over the lake below.

"*Monsieur,*" his voice was urgent. "The newspapers have now just arrived from Paris and they say that Tonchan was released from prison three days ago!"

There was a note in Pierre de Bethune's voice that brought Syrilla to a standstill.

She stood inside the open window of the salon and as she recalled the name, she could not help listening.

"Tonchan?" the Duc asked him. "Then his sentence must have been completed. It was for eight years, I remember."

"He is free, *monsieur*, and you must be very careful!"

The Duc did not reply and after a moment his Comptroller went on,

"You know that he swore to kill you!"

'That was a long time ago, Pierre. His temper has doubtless cooled while he has been in prison."

"I should think it most unlikely," Pierre de Bethune insisted. "He was indeed an animal, *monsieur,* a dangerous ferocious animal!"

He paused and Syrilla felt herself shiver as he finished,

"I can still hear Tonchon shouting at you from the dock. He sounded almost insane."

"He *was* insane," the Duc agreed. "But now he is free, Pierre, and there is nothing I can do about it."

"Except to take good care of yourself."

"What do you suggest I do?" the Duc asked.

It seemed to Syrilla that there was a note of amusement in his voice.

"I shall give instructions immediately to double the nightguards in the Château," Pierre de Bethune said. "I shall also have men and dogs patrolling the grounds. They will be armed and on my instructions, *monsieur,* they will shoot the moment they see Tonchon."

"I really think you are over-dramatising the situation, Pierre. Besides if he strangles me it would perhaps be poetic justice."

"You should not talk like that, *monsieur,*" Pierre de Bethune said sharply, "and I beg of you for the sake of Madame la Duchesse not to do anything foolhardy."

As if she could not listen any longer, Syrilla walked out onto the terrace.

At the sound of her footsteps both men turned round to look at her.

She ran towards the Duc.

"I overheard what you were saying," she said. "Oh, Monseigneur, you are in danger!"

"Pierre was exaggerating," the Duc replied calmly. "I am in no danger, Syrilla. This man has spent eight years in prison. He is not likely to wish to languish there for another eight!"

"B-but he – threatened you," Syrilla pointed out in a low voice.

"Men say many things when they are convicted of murder," the Duc remarked coolly.

"Why – why was he not – guillotined?" Syrilla asked in a low voice.

There was a moment's pause.

"It was a *Crime Passionnel* and the jury are usually sentimental about such a situation."

Syrilla would have spoken, but he interrupted.

"I have no wish to speak about it any longer. You would not have heard of this if Pierre had not come cackling to me like a mother hen. Forget it, Syrilla. Savigne is the safest place in the world as far as I am concerned and we can leave ourselves in Pierre's good hands."

He looked at his Comptroller meaningfully as he spoke and Pierre de Bethune knew that he was dismissed.

"Your pardon, *monsieur*, for mentioning the matter," he said. "I am well aware that I was unduly anxious."

He bowed as he moved away and Syrilla looked up at the Duc.

"Please, *Monseigneur*," she said, "you must be very careful. If anything should happen to you – my whole world would come to an end and I would – want to die!"

CHAPTER SIX

When dinner was finished and they had moved into the salon, Syrilla said to the Duc,

"Please tell me, *Monseigneur,* what you have done."

He knew what she referred to and, sitting down in a chair, he then told her,

"I dismissed the Manager of the vineyard and my Agent. They were both well aware of what was happening at Tauxise."

"I am so glad," Syrilla said. "I cannot bear to think of how those poor people must have suffered and there might well be others like them."

"I will take good care that this never occurs again," the Duc said firmly. "The Manager came to us from Bordeaux with a very big reputation, but I think in future I would be wise to entrust my vines to a local man who understands Touraine and our particular requirements."

"Papa always says that people who understand our local difficulties are better than those who come from other parts of France."

"Your father is very right," the Duc agreed, "and I hope in future, Syrilla, you will not be anxious about anything that is happening on the estate."

There was a silence and, looking at her expressive face, he knew at once that something was worrying her.

"What is it?" he asked.

She hesitated before she answered.

Then she said to him in a low voice,

"I would not wish to make – trouble."

"I think you have something to tell me," the Duc said, "and I want you to be frank with me, Syrilla."

Still she hesitated and he went on,

"After all you are now my wife and anything in this house or on the estate that concerns me also concerns you and is in part your responsibility."

"I had – forgotten that," she said simply,

"It is true," the Duc replied, "and now tell me what is worrying you."

"I know that I should not – listen to servants' gossip," Syrilla began in a low voice, "but they always talk – including, of course, my maid, Marie, when she is dressing me."

"I can understand that," the Duc smiled. "Gustave, my valet often lectures me!"

"Marie's brother works in the stables," Syrilla carried on, "and, when you are not here, the horses are often not – exercised and sometimes – neglected."

"What do you mean neglected?" the Duc asked sharply.

"I understand that your Head Groom is very old," Syrilla replied, "and in the winter he suffers from rheumatism. He therefore leaves everything to the under-groom who is a lazy man and at times the horses are skimpily fed and do not have water."

Syrilla did not look at the Duc as she spoke. She was so embarrassed at telling him that such things were happening because she felt that everything that concerned him should be perfect in every respect.

The Duc rose to his feet.

"*Curse it*!" he swore. "Why can I not be served properly?"

He sounded so angry that after a moment's hesitation Syrilla said,

"Mama said once that servants are like actors. They need applause, or in other words to be praised, otherwise they will feel that, if they do not have an appreciative audience, it is not worth giving a good performance!"

The Duc walked to the mantelpiece and stood with his back to her.

"What you are saying once again," he said, "is that my stables, like my vineyards, need my personal supervision."

"I did not wish to – upset you by telling you these things," Syrilla replied, "but then, of course, that is the truth. If the gardens look lovely and there is no one to say so, why should the gardeners take so much trouble?"

She paused and continued in a hesitating voice,

"If your horses are in very fine fettle and you are not – here to ride – them, who is to – care?"

She could not see the Duc's face, but she was very sure that he was scowling and, after a moment, she pleaded,

"Please don't be – angry with me saying – this, but you told me to be – frank with you."

"I want you always to tell me what you think is the truth," the Duc said, "and I believe you are always truthful, Syrilla."

"Of course," she answered, "and you know I would never lie to you of all people."

"You are unlike most women I know," he said cynically.

"That is not a compliment," Syrilla replied. "I realise how – inadequate and – dull I must be compared with the – brilliantly intelligent and – beautiful women you know in Paris."

There was a wistfulness in her voice that was somehow pathetic. The Duc seemed about to say something and then changed his mind.

"You have had a long day, Syrilla," he said, "and you must be tired. I suggest you now go to bed and we will talk about this in the morning."

"I would rather – stay and talk to – you now," she said quickly.

"Shall I say that I have very much to think about?" he said. "What has happened today has given me a great deal to consider and has perhaps turned my feet in a direction that they have never travelled before."

Syrilla did not understand, but she was too sensitive to press the point that she wanted to stay with him when she realised that the Duc wished her to go.

Instead she rose to her feet to stand beside him.

"I would like to tell you how – proud I was when I saw you riding into the village this morning," she said. "I told the villagers you would solve all their – problems, but I know that they did not really – believe me."

She paused and her eyes looked up at him admiringly as she went on,

"But you did come. You seemed to have a shining light about you and I knew that you would make them happy again."

"I told Pierre that you intended me to slay the dragon," the Duc said with a twist of his lips.

"That is what you certainly did," Syrilla smiled. "But I think, *Monseigneur*, there are other dragons that also require your attention."

She looked into his eyes as she spoke and now it seemed as if neither of them could look away.

Something Syrilla did not quite understand passed between them, she felt that her heart was beating frantically and had risen into her throat while her lips parted because it was hard to breathe.

Just for a moment it seemed as if everything had vanished except the Duc and they were alone on a high place in the sunshine.

Then he said almost curtly,

"Go to bed, Syrilla, and leave me to my thoughts."

He raised her hand to his lips and she curtseyed, but, as she went from the room, she was conscious only of the touch of his mouth against her skin.

*

Marie helped Syrilla to undress, then, when she got into bed, Marie blew out the candles and would have left the room but Syrilla asked her,

"Pull back the curtains over the centre window, Marie. It is still not too dark and I want to watch the stars coming out. Besides it is very hot."

"I'll do that, *madame*," Marie answered, "but I hope the light doesn't wake you up too early,"

"I wish to wake early," Syrilla replied, "there is so much to do."

She knew what she was really saying was that she wanted to be with the Duc.

When she was all alone, Syrilla stared at the translucent sky deepening to sable overhead where the first evening stars were like tiny diamonds.

Soon she knew that they would be reflected in the lake and she wondered if any place in the world could be as beautiful as the Château Savigne.

'Or any man so magnificent as its owner!' she whispered to herself.

She thought of the strange feeling she had felt in her heart when she had looked into his eyes as they had said 'goodnight'.

It was the truth when she had told him that, as he rode into the village where she was waiting so anxiously for him, it had seemed as if he was enveloped in a shining light.

She had thought for an instant that he was in the silver armour he had worn when she first saw him in the Tournament.

She had loved him then and now she realised it had been a child's love, the adoration she had felt through all

~151~

the next years had been for a mythical being, a Godlike creature who was not really flesh and blood.

Now she knew that the Duc was a man and she faced the fact that in the last few days her love for him had changed.

She had thought on her Wedding Day that she would indeed go on worshipping him as the embodiment of all that was very noble and fine, but somehow imperceptibly her love had changed until now when she saw him her heart leapt in a very different manner.

When he kissed her hand, she had known irrepressibly that what she yearned for was for him to kiss her lips.

'I love him! *I love him*!' she told herself, 'and I think the love I have for him now is that of a woman.'

She found herself pulsating with strange sensations she had never known and, because they were disturbing and a little frightening, she rose from the bed to go to the *Prie-Dieu*.

She knelt on the velvet cushion and put her hands together, palm to palm as she had done ever since childhood, bent her head and began the prayers that she had learnt at her mother's knee.

The conventional *Hail Mary* was said and then she prayed passionately to God to make the Duc love her because he needed and wanted her.

'Make him forget his other love,' she prayed. 'Make him think of me. Make him love me a little, just a little, as a man loves a woman.'

She had a feeling that perhaps she was wrong to ask such a thing and yet her whole being yearned for the Duc in a manner that was quite different from any emotion she had ever felt before.

Her body ached for him, her lips were soft and tender because they craved for his and she knew that her real idea of Heaven would be to feel his arms tight around her.

'I love him! *Oh, God, I love him!*' she said. 'Can love ever be wrong if it comes from You and is a part of You? I love him so much that he fills my whole world and there is nothing else but him.'

How long she prayed Syrilla had no idea, but her feelings were so intense that she felt God must hear them and that she poured her very life into her prayers.

Finally, when she felt almost exhausted by the effort that had involved every nerve in her body as well as every thought in her mind, she repeated the *Gloria* as her mother had taught her to do to end her prayers.

As she crossed herself, she heard a sound at the window.

As she said the last *Amen*, she vaguely thought that perhaps it was a bird or a bat seeking entry into the room.

She turned round, still kneeling on the *Prie-Dieu,* to see something so strange that for the moment she could not think what it was.

Half-blocking out the stars that now vividly filled the sky outside was a dark shadow.

As she stared at it, wondering what it could be, it seemed to come lower and lower until, when it reached the sill, the sky was almost completely obscured by it. Bewildered, but for the moment unafraid, Syrilla rose slowly to her feet.

Then the shadow came lower still and she realised that silhouetted against the stars she could see the body of a man!

With a sudden tension she remembered who it was and the danger it implied!

There was no need to enquire who it was entering the Château in such a way, who the shadowy figure sought and why.

With a cry of terror that came from her very heart she ran towards him.

*

The Duc sat for a long time in the salon until finally, as if he had found no conclusion to his thoughts, he went upstairs to bed.

His valet was waiting for him as was usual and, sensing that his Master had no wish to chatter, Gustave helped him undress and said nothing until he murmured respectfully from the door,

"*Bonsoir*, Monsieur le Duc."

The Duc did not bother to reply.

He left the candelabra alight and got into bed almost petulantly as if he defied himself to sleep. He knew even as he lay back against the pillows that he would not be able to do so.

He had wanted to think through his future plans tonight, but instead he had been haunted, despite every resolution, not to think of him, by Tonchon.

The scene in the dock kept coming back to him as vividly as if it had happened yesterday rather than nine years ago.

The Duc could hear his voice shouting wild obscenities, cursing him with every filthy oath that was used in the gutters of Paris and swearing that sooner or later he would kill him with his bare hands.

"You will die, my fine Duc!" he yelled as the *Gendarmes* dragged him away to the cells. "You will die as Zivana did, black in the face and gasping for air! You will die and your soul will rot in Hell!"

It was the ultimate climax to a trial that had been horrible and humiliating and which the Duc knew had changed his whole character and personality.

He had hoped that he would be able to forget and in his efforts to find forgetfulness he had plumbed the very depths of depravity and wallowed in filth which would have made any normal man's mind find ordinary thoughts an impossibility.

But he had been unable to erase from his consciousness and from his memory what he had learnt at the trial.

He remembered the first time that he had seen Jules Touchon.

The man had been performing in a 'turn' at the *Théâtre des Variétés* where Zivana was appearing in the ballet.

The Duc had thought at the time that Tonchon was a rather magnificent figure of a man and he learnt later that he had played many different parts in his life.

In his desire to reach the stage Tonchon had been an assistant to a lion tamer in a circus and he had also been an acrobat.

It was because of his fine looks that he was offered a small part by a touring company in the Provinces and as it had always been his ambition to become an actor he had left the circus to tour in France.

In course of time he played every male part in the company's repertoire until eventually he became the lead.

A talent-spotter from Paris noticed him and he was offered a leading part opposite an actress who had achieved fame, but was now far too old to hold the audience in a full-length play.

She could still, however, command a large salary for a sketch in one of the many variety theatres. The sketch received excellent reviews and she and Jules Torchon sometimes gave two or three performances at different theatres in one evening.

Although they had been in the same theatre, the Duc had no idea whatsoever that Zivana and Torchon had ever met.

Not until the trial did he realise that the secret of what they actually felt for each other had not only been kept from him but also from the elderly actress.

She was insanely jealous and expected her leading man not only to play the part of lover on the stage but also in her private life.

Almost as if he was watching a play portrayed in his bedroom, the Duc could see Jules Torchon acting his part, commanding the applause of every woman in the audience, then as the Judge passed sentence, see his face contorted with rage, shouting and screaming at him like a wild animal.

'I will not think about him – *I will not*!' the Duc told himself.

But he thought how often he had tried to thrust such memories away from him, turning in his extremity to drink and women and to the orgies that had taken place in his house in Paris and to the excesses that made many of his closest friends turn away from him in disgust.

Now when he had felt that he had almost forgotten Torchon's existence, the strangler had come back to haunt him.

Actually he was not afraid of what the actor might do to him physically. He could not believe that in a trial of strength he would not emerge the victor.

There was, of course, always a chance, as Pierre de Bethune feared, that Torchon might shoot him in a crowd or knife him in the back when he was least expecting it.

But there was no defence against such an attack, unless he had committed himself into a prison where he could be guarded day and night.

'If he kills me, what would it matter?' the Duc asked himself.

Then surprisingly he knew that he did not wish to die.

After the trial and the shock it had been to him, he wanted, if not to end his life, at least to change it completely.

If he had died in the process, he knew that he would not have cared.

And yet now, astonishingly, he wanted to live.

Life had never seemed at all precious to him before. He had never thought it to be of any particular consequence.

But if he had to live, he had thought he would enjoy himself and be *damned* to everyone else. Yet he wondered now in the darkness of his bedroom if the life he had led had brought him any enjoyment.

Had not some part of him always felt disgusted at the depravity that he had sunk into?

Had the bitterness and cynicism that invaded his mind to the point when looking back he thought he must have been at times a little mad, brought him anything but a dreadful sense of humiliation?

'Why should I think like this?' the Duc asked himself.

Why should the thought of Torchon being freed from his prison bring back the misery and revulsion that he had felt after the trial?

And yet it was hard to compare what he had felt then with what he felt now.

'I am older, I have no ideals left to be smashed and no more standards to lower,' the Duc thought savagely.

Yet now he wanted to live.

Quite suddenly it seemed to him that he had wasted the last nine years when there were so many other things he might have done with his time and money.

It was a thought that made him rise from his bed to pull back the curtains and look out of the window into the night.

He realised as he did so that he had not really looked at the lake and the gardens of the Château in starlight since he was a boy.

Then it had seemed to him something so lovely, so mystical and just so ethereal that his whole being had gone out in a desire to be a part of it.

At the same time he had the feeling of intense pride that this was his own Kingdom, his possession and he was a part of Savigne just as its history was a part of him.

He could see the stars reflected in the lake, a shimmer of silver on the still water and he could see the great trees in the Park silhouetted against the sky.

There was the fragrance of flowers on the air and he thought that he detected the scent of nightstock, which was one of his mother's favourite flowers.

When he had gone to see the Duchesse Douairière, he had known, although she was too tactful to say so, how thrilled she was that he was still at the Château and had not returned to Paris as he had intended to do.

For the first time since his boyhood there had been no need for words between them for they had each known what the other was thinking.

"You have made me very happy, Aristide," his mother said softly.

The Doctor had told the Duc that he was not to tire her and had warned him not to stay too long.

"Madame la Duchesse is better in health than I have known her to be for some time, but it would be a great mistake for her to become overtired."

"I will come and see you tomorrow, Mama," the Duc said and had known by the sudden light in her eyes that that was just what she wanted to hear.

He kissed her hand and felt her fingers tighten for a moment on his.

"God bless you, my dearest," she whispered.

Although he told himself it was absurd when he went from her room, he felt as if he had indeed been blessed.

The idea then suddenly came to him that, if anyone could save him from being haunted by Torchon, it would be his mother and Syrilla.

It would be their prayers that would prove a barrier between him and the demons that jeered at him and the ghosts that had haunted his soul for so long.

Then he told himself that even prayer could not save him from physical danger.

Then suddenly he had an acute feeling that suddenly danger was very near.

He could not explain it to himself, but it was there almost like a tingling, not so much in his mind as at the end of his fingers and at the back of his neck.

There was danger, a very considerable danger that was coming nearer to him, danger that threatened him physically.

It was so intense that the Duc turned from the window to open a drawer in the chest that stood beside his canopied bed.

It was a beautiful chest of rosewood inlaid with ivory and it was one of a pair that were very appropriate to the *Chambre du Roi*.

Lying in the top drawer was a loaded pistol.

The Duc had mocked himself for doing so, but he had loaded it when he came up to bed after Pierre de Bethune had told him that Torchon was now free.

Yet how could any man, however fanatical his desire to murder might be, break through the defences that the Duc knew that his Comptroller had surrounded the house with?

He had heard the tramp of the reinforced nightwatchmen making their rounds. He knew that out in the grounds the gamekeepers and the foresters had been given a rota by which they would patrol in three-hourly shifts the gardens, the Park and the woodlands.

'The whole thing is hysterical,' the Duc sighed scathingly. 'Pierre is just an old woman and I am a fool to listen to him.'

But however contemptuous he might be, he knew that the feeling of acute danger was still there.

It seemed to loom nearer and nearer and now, as if he could not help himself, the Duc opened the connecting door into the passage that led to Syrilla's room.

'I must think of her safety, if not of my own,' he told himself as an excuse for his own fears.

But there was no sound and he thought that he was just being nonsensical and the sooner he returned to bed the better.

'If I am going to feel like this every night,' he told himself, 'I shall go completely crazy!'

He stepped back into his own room and began to pull the communicating door to.

As he did so, he heard Syrilla scream.

It took the Duc just a very few seconds to run down the corridor to the door into Syrilla's room and, as he reached it, he heard her scream again.

He flung open her door and heard her cry frantically,

"You shall not hurt Monseigneur! You shall not kill him!"

He could see in the darkness a white patch that was Syrilla's nightgown as she struggled with someone big and dark against a background of the stars.

It was easy for the Duc to perceive the outline of a man's head and shoulders against the sky and to be aware that he was fighting with Syrilla.

Instinctively he knew, with a terror that pierced him like a knife, that Torchon's hands were at Syrilla's throat.

"Die! Die as Zivana died!" he heard the murderer shout in a voice that was like the snarl of a wild animal.

With the accuracy of an outstanding marksman the Duc shot him through the forehead.

Torchon fell back, his body thudding noisily to the floor and the Duc picked up Syrilla from where she had collapsed at his feet.

It was impossible to see her clearly, but his arms lifted her from the carpet and he carried her from the room without even a glance towards the man who he had just killed.

She was very light and he held her very close against him as he moved slowly down the connecting passage and into his bedroom.

He carried her to his bed and set her down on the pillows and, as her head lolled back against them, he wondered with a sudden constriction of his heart if she was dead.

The marks of Torchon's fingers were on her neck, her eyes were closed and he thought with a sudden terror that they were growing black as would happen if he had strangled her.

Frantically the Duc dragged at the bell-pull and then went back to kneel by the bed and put his ear against Syrilla's breast.

Her heart was beating, he could hear it and knew that she was alive if nothing else.

He pulled the velvet counterpane over her and then knelt down looking at her for a long moment before he rose to his feet to fling open the door to the corridor intending to shout for help.

But at that moment he saw his valet, hastily buttoning up his coat, come running towards him.

"Send for a Physician immediately!" the Duc cried out, "and tell Monsieur de Bethune to come here to me with all possible speed."

The sharpness of his voice and the abrupt way he spoke made the valet turn immediately and run back the way he had just come, but before he was half-way down the corridor Pierre de Bethune appeared.

"What is the matter?" he asked, as he moved towards the Duc, "I thought I heard a shot."

"You did," the Duc replied briefly. "I have killed Torchon! He was in Madame's room."

"How is that possible?" Pierre de Bethune gasped.

"I think that he must have come down from the roof on a rope," the Duc answered. "We might have remembered that he was an acrobat."

"My God!" Pierre de Bethune exclaimed.

The Duc was speaking over his shoulder as he was returning to his bedroom.

"And Madame?" Pierre de Bethune asked.

He followed the Duc and then saw Syrilla lying in the huge bed.

"He was attempting to strangle her," the Duc explained.

Pierre de Bethune said the words almost under his breath for in the candlelight Syrilla's cheeks were very white and her fair hair seemed to frame her face like a halo.

Just as the Duc had done, he knelt beside her and, taking her wrist in his fingers, felt for her pulse.

"She is alive!" he announced.

But he too could see the scarlet marks of the murderer's hands on her white throat and, as he turned to meet the Duc's eyes, they were both thinking of the brain damage that might have been inflicted.

The Duc picked up a candelabrum and carried it round the velvet curtains of the bed to look more closely at Syrilla's face.

He had thought in his first panic that her eyelids were growing black, but now he realised that it had only been a shadow.

There was no darkness underneath them and he gave a sigh of relief that seemed to come from the very depths of his being.

He put the candelabrum down again and said,

"Find out if they have already sent a groom for the Physician and make quite certain that devil is dead. I think I shot him through the forehead."

Pierre de Bethune did not speak.

He merely rose to his feet and went through the connecting door into Syrilla's bedroom.

The Duc knelt again at Syrilla's side and after a few moments he saw her eyelids flicker.

"Syrilla!"

His voice was unexpectedly low and hoarse.

It seemed for a long moment that she could not focus her eyes and, as he waited almost breathlessly for her response to his call, she saw his face and a faint smile touched her lips.

She tried to speak and failed. Then, as a little wavering hand crept towards her neck, the Duc said,

"Do not speak. That fiend has hurt your neck, but if you do understand what I say to you, just try to nod your head."

Her eyes were on his face as he asked,

"Are you in pain?"

Almost imperceptibly she shook her head and, as the Duc realised that his fears of brain damage were groundless, he took her hand and kissed it.

"Lie still," he said. "I have sent for the Physician. He will be here as quickly as possible. You must not try to move as it has been a great shock, but it is all over now."

He saw that she was trying to speak and knew without being told what she asked.

"I am safe," he said, his voice was very tender. "You were trying to save me, Syrilla, and you succeeded. I heard you scream and, as I came into your room, I saw you trying to protect me. I shot him, but not before he tried to strangle you."

He saw that she understood what he was saying. At the same time the marks on her neck seemed to deepen and he felt that she must be in some pain.

"If only I knew what to give you," the Duc said, "but I feel it would hurt you to drink."

Syrilla's fingers tightened on his and again he knew that all she really wanted was that he should be beside her and to be able to hold onto him.

"You are safe," the Duc insisted. "Safe now and for ever!"

It was what she wanted to hear and again she gave him a little smile.

Then his lips were on her hand lingering on the softness of her skin, kissing it again and again with a relief that he felt could only be expressed by some form of endearment.

*

Syrilla awoke to find the sunshine creeping golden into the room through the sides of the curtains and she thought that it must be very late in the day.

The events of the night slowly came back to her and she remembered vaguely the Doctor coming and giving her something to drink. It had been unpleasant, but it had sent her into a deep sleep.

Now she realised that she was not in her own room but in the Duc's.

She could see in the dim light the huge carved gold pelmets above the three windows and the lofty impressive furniture most unlike the delicately carved pieces in her own room.

Gradually the events of what had happened came back to her. She remembered trying to prevent Tonchon from attacking the Duc and feeling his fingers hard and frightening round her neck.

It had been a crazy thing to do, she thought, to try to prevent a large man from killing the Duc when she was weaponless and wearing nothing but a nightgown.

But she had been obsessed only with the idea of saving the man who she loved and had not for a moment counted the cost to herself.

Only when she thought she was dying and felt the breath being choked out of her did she send a despairing wordless cry to the Duc to save her.

And he saved her!

Vaguely, as she fell into a deep unconsciousness, she had heard a pistol shot and knew in her heart who had fired it.

Then she found him kneeling beside her, his face close to hers and he had kissed her hand, she could remember that!

Even though she still felt weak and limp and somehow far away from everything that was happening, his lips had the power to thrill her and she so wanted to go on listening to him talking to her.

'He is alive and we are together,' she mused.

Even if she was hurt and she could feel that her throat was well swollen, that was of no consequence beside the fact that the Duc was safe.

Now she only hoped that she was not disfigured for she wanted to look beautiful for him. With an effort, because she was still drowsy from the drug that the Doctor had given her, she put her hand up to her neck.

It was very tender and when she swallowed it hurt, but not as badly as it had done last night when the Doctor had made her swallow a potion that was extremely unpleasant to taste.

She next felt someone coming to the bedside and realised that she was not alone in the bedroom.

Then she saw Marie looking down at her.

"You are awake, *Madame*," Marie said. "The doctor told me I was to give you something to drink when you awoke, which will ease the pain in your throat."

She did not wait for Syrilla to answer, but produced a glass and, putting her arms round her Mistress's shoulders she raised her a little so that she could drink.

Whatever it was, it certainly did not taste as unpleasant as the drink she had been given the night before.

Syrilla thought that she could recognise honey and glycerine and remembered her mother giving them to her when, as a child, she had developed a sore throat.

Marie laid her back tenderly against the pillows and asked,

"Is there anything else you would like me to do for you, *Madame*? Don't try to speak but point and I'll understand."

Syrilla pointed to the curtains and Marie pulled them back and now the sunshine came flooding in and Syrilla looked around her.

It was the Duc's room! She thought that it was exactly the right background for him and she was in his bed!

She felt a thrill at the thought and then she told herself that it was just because he would have known she would not wish to sleep in the room where he had killed her attacker.

She was glad that Torchon was dead.

Now the Duc was safe and, thinking back, she knew how afraid she had been for him.

It seemed strange, she thought, that Torchon should have tried to strangle her and that she might have died the same way as Zivana.

The first crime had broken the Duc's heart and made him dedicate his life to the woman he had loved and whom he had gone on loving all through the years.

He would not have felt so strongly about her and yet perhaps he would have minded a little if she had died at the hands of the man he loathed and who had threatened his own life.

Torchon was dead, Syrilla thought, but Zivana still lived.

She had deliberately tried not to think of the locked room upstairs. Because she had been so happy in the Duc's company, she had let it lie at the back of her mind and her thoughts had shied away from it.

But now it was impossible not to recall that Zivana still lived on in this house, because she still lived in the Duc's mind.

His love was locked away with her somewhere in that most precious Shrine that only he entered and which was sacred to him.

For the first time in her life, Syrilla knew the pains of jealousy, a jealousy that seemed to stab her like a dagger and was far more painful than the marks on her neck.

She really wanted the Duc's love and she wanted him to think of her as a woman who was desirable and who attracted him as Zivana had done.

She had imagined that she could be content with friendship and companionship and the privilege of worshipping him as she had done as a child.

But it was not enough, not nearly enough!

The emotion she had felt as she rushed to defend him against an evil murderer was the passionate response of a woman who loved him as a man – and as her husband.

'*I want him*!' Syrilla thought. 'I want him here beside me. I want to be his wife. I want him to kiss me and touch me!'

Then almost as if an angel barred the way with a flaming sword, she knew that what lay between them and what would always lie between them was his love for a woman who was dead, a woman whose relics lay locked away in the Château and with them his heart.

It seemed to Syrilla at that moment as if she went down into a very special Hell of her own from which there was no respite or comfort.

She had known last night that she now loved the Duc quite differently from the way that she had loved him before.

Agonisingly it seemed as if her whole body burned for him and her whole being reached out towards him, longing for him, loving him so intensely that she felt it would be impossible to go on seeing him without confessing all that she felt.

Perhaps after all it would be best to do as his mother wanted and let him give her a child to carry on the title.

But even as she thought of it, her whole soul rebelled at the thought of his touching her when he wanted to touch another woman, of his kissing her when it would seem like dust and ashes on his lips, since he only wanted Zivana. Zivana! *Zivana!*

The name seemed to be haunting her until she could almost hear it spoken on the air and it was carried in on the wind.

She moved from side to side at the sheer intensity of her feelings without realising that she was doing so.

Now she heard Marie in a low voice say to someone at the door,

"I think *Madame* has a little fever, *Monsieur le Duc.*"

Syrilla was still and then she felt her heart turn over in her breast. Her eyes opened and they seemed to be filled with sunshine for the man who came across the room towards her.

"You are awake!" he said needlessly and, as her hands went out to find his, she managed to answer in a hoarse croaking voice very unlike her own,

"I-I am – all – right."

"You can speak! Oh, Syrilla, you can speak."

There was an expression of delight on the Duc's face that was unmistakable and Syrilla held onto him as if he was a lifeline that was pulling her back to safety and security.

"I-I am all – right," she whispered, "and – you are – safe."

"I am absolutely safe," the Duc answered, "and now all that matters is that you should get well quickly."

"I – feel well now that – you are – with me" Syrilla managed to say.

Her heart was singing because of the look in his eyes.

CHAPTER SEVEN

"Please, *monsieur*, let me get up. I feel quite well now," Syrilla pleaded.

The Doctor looked at her with a smile.

"Your mother-in-law, Madame la Duchesse Douairière, has already persuaded me much against my better judgement to agree to her travelling to Aix-les-Bains and then now you are bullying me into taking risks concerning yourself."

"*Belle-mère* is going away?" Syrilla asked in surprise.

The Doctor nodded.

"The Duchesse Douairière is very much better than she has been for some time," he said. "I think it is as much psychological as physical as she is so happy in her son's marriage."

Syrilla did not reply and after a moment he went on,

"She is very anxious to take the cure at Aix-les-Bains and I think that she also wishes to leave you two young people alone. So she is leaving tomorrow and, if she takes the journey in very easy stages, it should do her no harm."

"I am glad," Syrilla sighed.

She waited, her eyes on the Doctor, and after a moment he said,

"Very well, *Madame*, I suppose I must accede to your request. You may get up and go downstairs for an early dinner, but afterwards you are to come straight back to bed and rest tomorrow until I have seen you again. Is that agreed?"

"Yes – I agree."

There was a lilt in Syrilla's voice and a light in her eyes that the Doctor did not miss.

"You have been through a most unpleasant experience," he said, "but you are young, *Madame*, and have great courage. I think it will do you no permanent harm."

When he left her, Syrilla sat up in bed, planning in her mind what she would wear this evening for dinner with the Duc.

For two days the Doctor and the Duc had insisted that she must stay in bed and in fact the first day after what she had suffered at Torchon's hands she did feel dizzy and her throat throbbed almost intolerably.

But now it no longer hurt and, although the bruises had turned black and blue, she felt well in herself and only frustrated by the restrictions that were imposed upon her when she wanted so much to be with the Duc.

She knew at the back of her mind that she was afraid that, being alone and no one with him, he might find the Château so dull that he would want to return to Paris.

She had the feeling, although he had not said so, that he would not ask her to go with him and knowing what had happened in the past when he had been away for many years she felt somewhat apprehensive and worried.

It was not only this that made her just long to see him with an overwhelming intensity that seemed to grow hour by hour.

Having discovered her new love for him, it was hard to control her feelings when he came to her side to kiss her hand and ask her how she was and he stayed, it seemed to her, so short a time.

It was difficult not to embarrass him by telling him fervently how much she loved him, how she longed for him to put his arms around her.

How, she asked herself, could he have carried her from her own room to where she was now without her being aware of it?

Because the Duc thought that she would not wish to return to her own bedchamber so soon after a man had been killed there, she had been left in the *Chambre du Roi*.

Every time she looked around her it brought the Duc so vividly to her mind that it was almost as if he lay beside her and she could touch him.

Marie, who had come into the room after the Doctor had left, broke in on her thoughts.

"Monsieur le Medecin says to me that you may rise, *Madame*, and dine downstairs," she announced. "That is good news, very good news, but I think when he sees Monsieur le Duc he'll insist on dinner bein' early."

"I would like it early," Syrilla replied.

As far as she was concerned, the earlier the better then she could be with the Duc again.

She could look at him, listen to him and perhaps whatever the Doctor said they would be able to sit alone for a little while in the salon when dinner was finished.

"What will you wear, *Madame*?" Marie asked – and that, of course, was an absorbing subject, which took them a long time to decide.

Syrilla discarded one gown after another and when at length she had had her scented bath and was dressed she wondered at the last moment if one of her other gowns would have been a better choice.

But in fact the gown she wore could not have been more becoming.

Of pink tulle, made with the skill that could only have come from Paris, the full skirt billowed out from her tiny waist and the tight bodice revealed the curves of her breasts.

There was a lace bertha embroidered with stars that twinkled with diamanté, a draped skirt that was caught up with constellations of stars and there was a cluster of them on each of her small satin shoes.

"*C'est ravissante, Madame*," Marie exclaimed. "It's the most beautiful gown I've ever seen."

Syrilla smiled and equally she was wondering whether the Duc would think it beautiful.

Having lived in Paris, he must have seen women wearing so many fabulous and exciting gowns, they could never mean the same to him as they meant to her and Marie who had never travelled outside Touraine.

Her neck remained a problem.

The bruises were still very prominent against her white skin and she was afraid that the Duc would think them ugly.

Also it would remind him of what she had suffered and so he would insist that she must return to bed as quickly as possible.

There were many diamond and pearl necklaces in her jewel box, some of which had been Wedding presents and some of which belonged to the Savigne family. But she thought that they were too heavy and also might draw attention to what she wished to conceal.

Instead she and Marie arranged a thin piece of tulle round her neck and fastened it on one side where the bruises were worst with two small white orchids, which had been included in one of the vases of flowers that decorated her room.

The flowers gave her a very young fresh look and she wore no jewellery. Her thin fingers were ornamented only with her Wedding ring.

Syrilla took a last look at herself in the mirror and then turned towards the door.

"Tonight, *Madame*, I think you would like to sleep in your own bedroom?" Marie asked as she reached it.

Syrilla hesitated for a moment.

"Yes – that would be best. I am sure that Monsieur le Duc wishes to return to his own bed."

She wondered for a brief moment if the ghost of Torchon would haunt her and whether she would have to re-live that moment when she had seen his dark body descending outside the window and not known what it was.

Then she told herself that it would be stupid and ill-bred of her to be afraid. Besides the Duc would be next door and, if she called out to him, she was certain that he would hear her.

She felt herself quiver at the thought and then told herself that she would never call him unless it was really urgent. If he came to her just out of courtesy or consideration, it would be worse than if she faced her own fears alone.

She went slowly downstairs to find the Duc waiting for her in the salon.

She saw, as she walked towards him, the glint of admiration in his eyes that she always looked for.

Her heart was beating frantically and she felt that strange and wonderful excitement seep over her because they were alone.

"This will not prove too much for you?" he asked in a low voice.

"No, of course not," she answered. "I wanted to get up yesterday, but the Doctor would not agree to it."

"He is being sensible on my instructions," the Duc said. "You must take things very easy for a few days."

"Yes, of course," Syrilla agreed a little coyly.

She had a strange feeling that their lips were saying one thing while their thoughts were really quite different.

She could not explain it to herself, but she felt as if she vibrated to something that the Duc was feeling, which she could not understand, but yet it was very wonderful.

He gave her his arm and escorted her into dinner.

While the servants were waiting on them, bringing them in delicious dishes that were far too numerous for Syrilla, the Duc talked to her about the estate, of his plans for the vineyards and the visit he had made that afternoon to Tauxise.

"They are happier?" Syrilla asked.

"Thanks to you I have never met a more happy and contented collection of people," he answered. "The men are working hard dragging up the old vines, the women were washing and sewing and the children's faces were scrubbed so clean so that they seemed to shine like copper pans!"

Syrilla laughed.

"I am sure they resented that treatment!"

"I have promised that, when you were well enough, you would pay Tauxise a visit. They speak of you as if you were a Saint sent from Heaven to help them."

"They should not do that," Syrilla protested. "It made me feel most embarrassed when the women knelt and touched my skirt."

"You performed a miracle," the Duc said, "and they will never forget it."

He paused and then added quietly,

"Neither shall I forget what you have done for our people."

She felt the colour come into her cheeks and her eyes fell before his. Then almost as if it was an effort the Duc talked of other things until dinner was finished.

They went back to the salon and now, because she was afraid that he would send her to bed, Syrilla went to the open window to look out into the garden.

As it was so early, the sun was only just sinking into a blaze of crimson and gold behind the trees in the Park and it was reflected in the lake, which was also gold, while the shadows on the lawn were purple.

It made such a beautiful picture that Syrilla drew in her breath.

"Could any place be as lovely as this?" she enthused.

"That is what I have often thought myself," the Duc said, "but, Syrilla, I want to talk to you."

There was a note in his voice that made her turn quickly and look at him apprehensively.

There was something solemn in the way he spoke and she had a sudden fear that he was about to tell her that he was going away.

Because she was so nervous, she clasped her hands together and she knew that the Duc was feeling for his words.

After a moment he said,

"On the very first night of our marriage, Syrilla, you told me that you had overheard two people saying that I had a secret locked room in the Château."

He paused and, feeling that he expected her to answer him, she said in a frightened little voice.

"Y-yes – I heard that."

"You suggested, I remember, that it was a Shrine where I had locked away my heart."

~181~

Again he looked at her and now it was impossible for Syrilla to say above a whisper,

"Yes – that is what I – thought."

"I want you to come with me to that room," the Duc said, "and see what it contains. It is in fact a Shrine to my love."

Syrilla felt as if she had been turned to stone.

Instead of her heart beating excitedly, she thought that it had suddenly become frozen and there was ice creeping into her veins and paralysing her to the point where it was hard to think.

She tried to speak, but no sound would come from between her lips,

"Will you come with me now?" the Duc asked gravely.

She nodded and they walked across the room side by side. He stopped only to pick up a key from the writing desk as he passed it.

'What can this mean?' Syrilla asked herself frantically.

Why was he suddenly showing her the locked room that he had dedicated to Zivana's memory and which she had tried to forget ever since their marriage?

She thought with a sudden terror that perhaps he was going to explain to her once again that Zivana meant everything to him and he could no longer bear her to be his wife.

'He means to get rid of me,' Syrilla thought and felt as if a thousand knives cut her into pieces and the pain of it was almost unbearable.

They walked in silence up the Grand Staircase and then the Duc turned and led the way along the corridors towards a part of the Château that Syrilla had never seen because she had learnt that the rooms were not in use.

As they then reached what she knew must be the end of the house, they climbed another staircase and she guessed that they were going to one of the turrets.

When they reached the top, there was a landing with one door and Syrilla knew that she was right. This was one of the large turrets of which there were four, one at each corner of the Château.

The Duc handed her the key he held in his hand and then stood to one side.

She took it from him automatically and so, knowing what he now expected her to do, she felt that it was impossible to obey him.

All the jealousy she felt for the dead woman seemed to well over her in a flood-tide to leave her shaking and at the same time afraid as she had never been afraid before.

How could there be any chance of her competing with a woman who had held a man's love for nine years after she was dead – a woman who had become sacred and the symbol of everything that was desirable and perfect and yet was lost?

But because Syrilla was incapable of expressing what she was feeling, because she felt as if she was only a puppet which must obey the Duc, she inserted the key in the lock.

Although it looked heavy, it turned easily as if it had recently been oiled.

Just for a moment Syrilla hesitated. Then, as the Duc did not move, she pushed the door open.

At a first glance she was surprised that the turret-room was so large.

The floor was carpeted and the sunlight was coming in through the open windows. But that was not the only light in the room.

There were candles, large candles in gold candlesticks burning on either side of a picture and surrounded on both sides by flowers.

They were white and Syrilla could smell the fragrance of lilies, roses and carnations as she moved towards the end of the room feeling as if her feet were weighted down with lead.

But the picture the candlelight shone onto was not, as she expected, that of a stranger.

It was a portrait of herself!

She recognised it instantly for it was the one that her father had always liked of her and which he had presented to the Duc on their marriage.

She stared at it in bewilderment. Then, with her eyes wide and frightened, she turned to look at the Duc.

He was standing just a step behind her and he then said,

"You wished to see what was enshrined in my heart."

For a moment Syrilla did not understand him. Then, as the ice within her breasts seemed to melt and a strange and wonderful feeling crept over her, the Duc said abruptly in a voice that was surprisingly harsh,

"I have a great deal to tell you, Syrilla. Sit down."

She looked at him in perplexity and she then saw a damask-covered chair near her and sat down feeling as if her legs would no longer carried her.

Her mind was in a turmoil and yet because of what the Duc had said and, as her portrait was the only object in the room, she felt as if her eyes were blinded by the candlelight and there were the strains of music sounding in her ears.

The Duc walked to the open window to lean against it.

"You had heard a story on the very day of our marriage," he began, "that I had loved a ballerina called 'Zivana Mezlanski' and that when she was strangled I had all her belongings brought here to set them up in a Shrine to her memory."

He did not look at Syrilla as he was speaking, but at her portrait surrounded by candles and flowers.

He seemed to be waiting for her to speak and after a moment she said,

"I told – you that was – what I – had heard."

"It was true," the Duc said. "I was twenty-one when I met Zivana and I thought that she was the most exquisite dancer and the most beautiful woman I had ever seen."

His lips tightened for a moment as he went on,

"I fell in love with her or rather I was infatuated, as only a young idealistic man could be, with a woman from a very different world to the one that he had always lived in."

Syrilla clasped her hands together.

There was a pain in his voice as he spoke, which was echoed in herself.

"I had known so few women intimately before I had met Zivana and certainly no women who lived the life she did. I thought she was so perfect in every way that I wanted to make her my wife."

He drew in his breath.

"I wanted her to marry me immediately and come back here to live with me at Savigne."

Syrilla wondered why he was telling her this. She knew it was hurting him to speak of the past and she tried not to think of her feelings but of his.

"Zivana made many excuses why we should not be married at once," the Duc went on, "and she became my mistress, although in reality I felt it was a sacrilege against the greatness and sanctity of our love."

He paused before he added almost violently,

"I was such a fool, Syrilla, an ignorant young fool who knew nothing about the realities of life!"

His voice seemed to echo round the room, before with an effort, he went on in a quieter tone,

"Zivana put me off with promises that she would marry me once she had finished her contract at the theatre when she had had just one more Season with the ballet. It was excuses, always excuses, and I accepted them because there was nothing else I could do."

The Duc was silent for a moment.

Then he said,

"How was I to know that they were all lies? Lies that I was gullible enough to believe without question."

Syrilla made a little gesture as if she wished to comfort him, but he continued,

"You know what happened. She was strangled by Jules Touchon and I found her lying dead on the floor of her dressing room."

"It – must have been a – terrible – shock for you," Syrilla whispered.

"I think I became a little insane," the Duc replied, "because I believed that if I had not been delayed in leaving the auditorium after her performance was over I might have reached her dressing room earlier and therefore saved her from her assailant's hands."

"You – knew who had – killed her?"

"One of the other performers had seen Touchon leaving Zivana's dressing room," the Duc replied, "and when he subsequently disappeared it was obvious who her murderer had been."

"But they – caught – him?"

"Not for six months," the Duc answered. "During that six months I mourned Zivana as the woman who would have been my wife."

The Duc had not looked at Syrilla since he had started to speak and she thought that it was because he could not bear to think of her taking the place of Zivana whom he had loved with all his heart.

"Then Touchon was caught," the Duc went on.

Now he spoke quickly as if he wished to come to the end of his story.

"He was brought to trial and it was then that I learnt the truth."

"The – truth?" Syrilla asked wonderingly.

"He had been Zivana's lover and it was he she cared for and not me!"

"Oh – *no*!" Syrilla whispered beneath her breath.

"Her letters to him were read out in Court," the Duc continued. "They revealed that the Zivana I imagined I knew had never existed. She was a wild uncivilised Russian obsessed by a man because he was rough and brutal, a man who treated all women as chattels and had no use for them except physically."

There was so much bitterness in the Duc's voice that Syrilla felt it was almost unbearable to continue to listen to him.

She did not know that he was hearing again the letters that had been read out in Court as an extenuating reason for Touchon's crime.

Letters so passionate, so burning with violence and desire, that they held everyone in the Courtroom spellbound while the Duc had felt humiliated into the dust.

Zivana had even referred to him in her outpourings.

"Touchon is very young and therefore knows nothing about love," she had written almost contemptuously, *"but he is very rich and we need the money. But, oh, the agonies of being with him when I might be with you! I lie in his arms wondering who you are and I want you and need you, my whole body yearns and burns for you!"*

There had been dozens of letters written frantically by a woman who loved a man with a deep-seated Slavonic passion that made her veer between deepest of depressions and wild exhilaration.

The letters revealed that Touchon had beaten her and knocked her about as he was so jealous and that she had gloried in his brutality.

She loved him, at the same time, as she said over and over again, the Duc was rich and they both needed everything that she could extract from him.

But money had not assuaged Touchon's jealousy.

In a fit of rage, when they must have quarrelled over the fact that she had another lover besides himself, he had strangled her.

The case had taken days while the Duc had passed through an indescribable Hell.

When the verdict was brought in as *Crime Passionnel*, he had changed from an idealistic youth to a man so cynical and bitter that there was nothing but hatred left in his heart.

Now he turned his back on Syrilla and stood still looking out of the turret window with unseeing eyes.

"I am not going to tell you of my life in Paris during the last eight years," he said. "You would not understand and, God knows, I have no wish for you to do so."

He paused for a moment.

"But I want you to know that I was far from doing all the noble work that you envisaged. Instead I was committing every crime against decency that it is possible to ever imagine. I had been hurt and I wanted to hurt."

His lips tightened before he added,

"With every woman I met I tried to avenge myself on Zivana. I hated them and yet I used them for my own needs. If I ruined their lives or left them weeping and unhappy, it pleased me. Because I had been wounded and scarred, or so I believed, I wanted to crucify them!"

The hurt in his voice was very obvious and Syrilla was more aware of that than of the words he spoke.

"The way I behaved was a disgrace to my name and the noble traditions of my family," the Duc went on. "People remonstrated with me, but I laughed at them."

He drew in his breath before he carried on,

"No one will have told you the truth, Syrilla, but I have become a byword for all that is low and bestial, a man who is utterly debauched, a man who has dragged a noble title into the gutter and smeared it with mud."

There was so much self-condemnation in the way he spoke that Syrilla felt tears come into her eyes.

He obviously did not expect her to answer him and, after a second's silence, he said,

"When my mother asked me to marry for the sake of the continuity of the family, I told her I would have no part in choosing my bride. I meant to stay here one night and one night only and then return to the gutters I had come from."

Now Syrilla found her voice.

"Then – why did – you not do – so?"

"Because you were different from everything I had imagined still existed in the world," he answered. "Because you believed in me, because you brought back dreams that I thought I had lost nine years ago. Dreams of a woman who could be so innocent and pure and inspire a man spiritually as well as physically."

"And then?" Syrilla asked.

"I fell in love with you!" he replied. "I fought against it, make no mistake about that. I fought against everything you stood for, everything you are, but when I saw you struggling with Touchon, when I carried you in my arms and thought you were dead, I knew that I had lost my heart completely and irretrievably as I have never lost it before."

His voice deepened as he continued,

"I knew then that what I had felt for Zivana was the infatuation of a youth who had no knowledge of life and little sense of values. What I feel for you, Syrilla, is very different. I love you as a man with my heart and with my mind and, if I had one, which I doubt, my soul."

He made a gesture with his hand.

"You fill up the whole of my life to the exclusion of all else. You are everything that is perfect. But I know only too well that I am utterly unworthy of you."

Syrilla made a little sound, but it did not interrupt him.

"After the despicable manner in which I have behaved these last years, I am not certain if there is a way back even for a '*sinner who repenteth*'."

There was intense passion in his words as he went on,

"I want you, Syrilla, I want you unbearably as my wife, my real wife. But what have I to offer you? I am certainly not the Knight you believe me to be, the hero who has no existence except in your imagination!"

The Duc paused and then he said cynically,

"I am not even certain that the love I have for you is clean, knowing the foul creature that I have become!"

He drew in his breath, before he said almost as if it was a challenge,

"The answer is up to you. If you will take me as I am, I swear I will try to become what you want me to be. But I will not lie to you, I do *not* wish you to have any illusions about me. If you behave as you should, you will shrink away from me as something beyond the pale, a man with whom you could have nothing in common. The choice is yours."

The Duc's voice seemed to die away and there was a silence in the room.

It was a silence so acute that Syrilla felt as if she was no longer breathing and the Duc too seemed to be holding his breath.

Then suddenly she was at his side.

Without turning he heard a little voice say,

"Will you – tell me why – after we were married – even though I told you what I felt – you did not make me your – wife as you had – intended?"

"That is what I meant to do," the Duc replied, "but the first night I was too surprised by what you told me to have words to answer you. The second night when I came to your room you were praying and I knew that I could not spoil or hurt anything so pure and perfect."

He heard Syrilla draw in her breath.

Then she said,

"That was exactly how the – Knight in whom I believed would have – behaved – but just as you have changed and you say your – love for me is – different from anything you have ever felt before – so too is mine."

The Duc was listening to her intently, but he did not speak and after a moment she said very softly,

"I love you now not as my *Monseigneur*, not as someone dedicated to an ideal, but as a man! I love you, Aristide, and I long to be your – wife, your real wife – if you want me."

The Duc turned from the window.

"Want you?" he asked. "God knows I want you. But have you thought, Syrilla, about all I have told you?"

"Why should I think about it?" she asked. "To me you have always been everything that is – noble and fine. What happened in the – past does not concern – me. I want to be part of your future – a future in which if you – love me as I love you, we can be – together here at Savigne."

She saw the Duc's eyes light up and, although he did not move or touch her, she felt as if he drew nearer to her.

"Do you understand what you are saying?" he asked. "I love you, Syrilla, I love you as I swear I have never loved anyone in the whole of my life! But you will have to teach me to find again all the things that you believe in and which once very long ago were mine."

There was something almost pathetic as he added,

"I have lost them and without them I am so afraid that I shall not be able to make you happy."

"All I – want is – you."

Now, as if she could not help herself, Syrilla put out her arms and, as she did so, the Duc pulled her almost roughly against him and looked down at her face raised up to his.

"I love you! I adore you! *I worship you!*" he said. "Help me, Syrilla, to change myself back to the man you have believed in all these years, but who is not worthy even to kiss the ground you stand on."

"You are – everything I ever – dreamed of – or wanted," Syrilla whispered.

The Duc drew her closer and then, almost as if he was afraid to touch her, his lips sought hers.

It was a very gentle kiss, the kiss of a man who is pulsatingly aware of something sacred and approaches it with reverence.

Then, as their lips met, the wonder of it seemed to Syrilla to envelop them both with a blinding light that came not from the sky but from within their own hearts.

She felt herself drawing closer and yet closer to the Duc and her body melted against his until they were no longer two people but one.

She felt her lips responding to the insistence of his and a flame flickered within her that seemed to run through her veins with an ecstasy and a glory beyond anything she had ever dreamt of or imagined.

'I love you! *I love you!*' she wanted to say, but it was impossible to speak.

She only knew that the Duc held her captive and at the same time it was as if in his kiss he dedicated himself, knowing that he asked from her that which she could only give in love.

When finally he did raise his head to look at her shining eyes, her cheeks flushed with happiness and her breath coming quickly from between her lips, he made a sound that was half an exclamation of triumph and yet also a groan of contrition.

"You are so beautiful, my precious darling, so perfect in every way. I have told you that I am not worthy of you and yet I love you so completely and so absolutely that I cannot ever let you go."

"I have – belonged to you – already for – nine years."

"Why did I not know? Why did I not feel your sublime love reaching out to save me from myself?"

"Perhaps, because – you have – suffered, our love will seem more – precious and more – wonderful."

His arms tightened about her.

"I might well have lost you!" he said. "If that fiend had killed you as he tried to do, there would be nothing left for me but to die in degradation and as quickly as possible."

"You were not meant to – die any more than I – was," Syrilla answered. "I think because – there is so much for you to do. You are – wanted here. Your people need you. I – need you! I want to be with you always and – forever!"

"That is what we will be," the Duc promised. "But, oh, my darling little love, you must help me so that the crimes I have committed can all be forgotten and people will once more respect the name of Savigne because you adorn it with all your glory and beauty."

"We will do all that is expected of us – together," Syrilla said, "but you do love me – you really do love me?"

It was the cry of a child who wants to be reassured and the Duc kissed first her forehead, then both of her eyes before he said,

"It will take me a lifetime to tell you how much I adore you and to make you as happy as I mean to do. But now, my precious lovely one, you must obey the Doctor's instructions and go to bed."

"I – want to – stay with you – I cannot – leave you," Syrilla whispered.

The Duc smiled and his lips were very close to hers as he asked,

"Who said anything about my leaving you?"

Syrilla felt her heart leap. Then almost as if she was afraid that she had not heard him aright she whispered,

"You mean – ?"

"I mean that you are my wife," the Duc said, "and, my sweetheart, there will be no more barriers, no more secrets, no love locked in. We will be together as we were meant to be since the beginning of time and I will teach you to love me as I love, adore and worship you."

"That is just – what I want," Syrilla murmured. "That, my darling wonderful Aristide, is what I have been – praying for."

"Then why are we waiting?" the Duc asked.

He picked her up in his arms as he spoke.

With his lips holding hers completely captive he carried her close against his heart down the stairs from the turret leaving the door wide open behind them.

There were angels singing and their love was to be for Eternity and beyond.